The Strange and the Wonderful

AN ANTHOLOGY OF THE PASSING PLACE

Mark Hayes

Steampowered Books

Steampowered Books
11 Saltholme Close
Middlesbrough
UK
TS2 1TL

Publisher's Note: This is a work of fiction. Names, characters,
places, and incidents are a product of the author's imagination.
Locales and public names are sometimes used for atmospheric
purposes. Any resemblance to actual people, living or dead, or
to businesses, companies, events, institutions, or locales is
completely coincidental.

Mark Hayes. -- 1st ed.
ISBN ISBN-13: 9798852779403

For my father,
who has passed beyond the cares of this world.

The last bouncers been pitched at the man in the
crease
The last putt has been sunk on the 18th
The last bowl sent to jack, over the crown
The games are all done, the sun has gone down

In what comes after, may there be fields of play
Where no quarter is asked, given, nor received
And after each game, no matter who won
There'll be drinks at the bar, laugher and fun

For all the smiles that you gifted
All the mischievous winks
And all the joy that you gave us
As Husband, Dad, Grandad, John…

Esqwith's Passing Place, a bar that sits on the edge of many realities and is part of none. A place people stumble into some times and tell stories to Richard the piano player, Morn the green haired girl, the grey-man who mops the floors, the chef who knows what you want before you order it, Lyal behind the bar, Sonny the philosophical bouncer, but mostly they tell them to Esqwith herself, and of course the cat.

These are some of those stories, but we'll begin with a story of the inhabitants of the bar itself, a tale of the strange and the wonderful...

Contents

THE STRANGE AND THE WONDERFUL

A minor interlude from the Passing Place

8   Mark Hayes

Colour was a strange and wonderful thing. The strangest and the most wonderful of things, Greyman considered as he pushed his mop over a particularly stubborn sticky patch on the barroom floor. He often found himself wondering if colour had always been there? All the rich vibrancy of life obscured by an ever-present grey mist that had perpetually hung before his eyes.

He could remember exactly when colour had entered his life. Sat in his grey cubicle, in the grey offices, of a grey ministry, of the grey world, in the middle of what could only be described as a grey day, in a grey month, of a grey year, in a grey life. It had been the moment he had opened a grey file that crossed his desk, a grey file which contained his own name. The moment the grim monotony of existence had come to a head and he'd found himself staring at that form, facing a choice he did not understand, had never understood, accept or deny. He had sat there, staring at that open file for what may have been an age.

Paralysed by both indecision and a realisation of the pointlessness of his existence.

But then, he'd heard a sound.

A sound that stood out amid the humdrum of the office. Amid the shuffling papers, the hammering of stamps, the pushing of files, scratching of pens, the haggard rasping breaths of his colleagues and the weighted sighs of the grey bureaucracy at work.

A sound that was at once both out of place and down at his feet.

The sound was a word half purred, half meowed and anything but grey.

"Coming?"

His surprise at this unexpected development, in a place where nothing unexpected ever occurred, Grey-man had torn his gaze away from the file before him and looked down to see a tortoiseshell cat weaving its way between the forest of desk and chair legs. A cat, any cat, in the grey offices was remarkable enough, but what had caught his gaze and threw him out of his strange catatonia was the ginger segments of the cat.

Bright luxuriant orange red patches of fur.

Bright orange red fur that were the first colours he had ever seen.

She'd come to a standstill beside his desk, looking up at him in turn and staring back into his eyes. A small furry face full of inquiry and challenge, and his world stood still once more.

Then the cat cocked her head just a little to the side, and 'spoke' her question again, if spoke was the right word for a question he did not hear exactly, except in the back of his mind.

"Coming..?"

And then, with that pointed question hanging behind her, she'd turned and prowled down the worn grey carpet of the walkway between the endless rows of grey cubicles. Leaving him sitting there, watching her go, a strange new thing in a world that never changed. A thing of shades, pigments and colour… Unsure if he even dared follow, unsure of his sanity, as that most terrible of all fears gripped him, the fear of the unknown.

And then, as he'd watched, he saw a third remarkable thing. With each step she took, her paws would disturb the layers of dust upon the carpet in a way the shoes of the workers never did. Throwing up tiny puffs of dust behind her and leaving fresh paw prints of clean red shag-pile beneath. Little circles of colour where no colour had ever been.

It was those little circles of red that had made his mind up. There was something so impossibly beautiful about them, he had to follow…

The cat had led him to the doorway. The same doorway he entered the everyday at 9.00am. No matter when that 9.00am was. As she'd vanished through it, he'd followed, like a child following a piper, through the doorway, to be greeted with another surprise, another strange miracle. The door he'd passed through, as he had hundreds of times before, opened not to the shabby grey stairwell he had expected, but into a new world of a thousand pigments and none of them grey…

Often he found himself thinking of that last day in the grey world. Usually when he was doing some task others would find mundane. Yet he would find himself, smiling. Smiling at the joy of rainbows in soap bubbles as he washed dishes, or the way his mop would leave those self-same rainbows on the barroom floor as the light refracted through the water that trailed behind the mop head.

Light, he had come to conclude, was the thing, a magic thing.

Light made the grass in Morn's garden green. Light gave colour to the spirit bottles behind the bar. The blue of curacao, the green of Absinthe, the cheery red of the bar top, even the polished white of Richard's piano. Light made all the colours, colours so bright to his eyes. Light was wonderful.

Colour was wonderful.

He ran the mop over the stubborn patch on the floor once more. The patch between the bar and the pool table, which always seemed to require a little extra mopping. Not that he minded this so much, as mopping this patch afforded him the best view of the kitchen service door. So he never questioned why he always found himself having to give it an extra couple of swipes of the mop. Certainly he could not conceive the possibility that someone was arranging things that way, it was to him no more than a happy coincidence. One that allowed him a chance to look up and occasionally catch a glance of Jolene bustling in and out of the kitchen. A glance which, if she caught him doing so, always led to a smile crossing her lips. A smile he would return in kind.

He was not sure why…

At this particular moment, as he looked up from his mop to glance in the direction of the service hatch, he found himself experiencing a moment of disappointment as this time he did not catch sight of her. He was not sure where that disappointment came from any more than why her smile brought one to his lips.

In truth, as much as he found joy in the strange new world of colour he called home, he was sure he would never truly understand all its facets, any more than the endless array of colours he found himself noticing, most of which he could not even name.

And then there were those other colours, the ones he could not see at all, but rather felt. The ones inside him, the ones that burst upon him without warning. The colours he had come to recognise as emotions.

The troublesome patch thoroughly mopped, he

moved on once more, a strange blue feeling of disappointment within him, though it started to fade as his eyes followed the rainbows his mop made out of soap suds on the floor. Watching the greens and gentle reds of joy flowing as light danced across the surface, he found his smile once more. All the while not realising he was moving in time to the tune coming from the piano. His progress around the barroom an odd little dance with his mop as a partner, all the while unwittingly humming a tune he could not name.

He could never give name to a tune, music another new and wonderful thing, another thing of colour.

Everything was colour…

Then, as he waltzed across the bar floor he heard it, the most delightful sound, and the strangest thing of all.

'Tick' it went…

He stopped his mopping and found himself looking up at the grandfather clock that sat in the middle of the barroom's wall.

'Tock' it continued…

And for a moment he rested, leaning on his mop, eagerly watching the second hand's slow relentless progress around the clock face.

'Tick' it went again…

This was the strangest music to his soul. A counter point to the piano. Relentless in its wonder.

'Tock' it sang.

The clock always caught him unawares, every time he came to it, another little miracle in the world of colours, the world of miracles…

"Why do you do that, hun?" said a voice behind

him, rich with the dulcet tones of the mid-west, drawing him out of his revelry.

He turned towards the voice, towards her, and found a smile coming unbidden to his lips. Though the colours inside him were confused, he did not know how to reply. Words were not his forte to begin with. All the less so when it came to speaking with Jolene. So instead he just smiled at her.

"Not a day goes by I don't see y'all staring at that clock, off in a world of your own…" Jolene continued when he failed to reply.

He wondered, worriedly, if she was scolding him, making a jest, or just being friendly. Greyman struggled with understanding the emotions in others even more than he struggled with understanding them within himself. As such, his smile began to falter, turning into a frown.

"Hey now, y'all don't pay me no mind, I was just wondering what you found so damn fascinating about that there clock is all," she said, her expression hardening momentarily before she gave him a broad reassuring smile. Which is to say he found it reassuring and that he was almost sure that was her intent. Besides, she had the most wonderful cherry red lips even when she was not smiling. Lips which made the colours inside him feel odd, in a nice way. The bright shade of her lip-gloss seemed full of vivacious intent. But then Jolene was, to his eyes, an explosion of colour. Her strawberry blonde beehive hair, the light pink of her blush, the bright yellow of her circa 1960's waitress uniform and the deep dark blues she wore as eyeshadow that framed her full of life eyes.

Her eyes, which sparkled so.

Eyes of a rich hazel…

'Hazel', that was a new one he realised, a new colour he could name… And with this realisation he found himself smiling back at her once more. While at the same time he had to force himself not say the new word out loud and feel how the name of the colour rolled over his tongue.

Occasionally he wondered where the names of colours came from. Occasionally, and more often of late, he was sure, he would find them popping into his head, as if they had always been there. And each time that happened he found a whole new level of delight at the discovery.

"Now that's better, hunny, you know what they say, smile and the world smiles with y'all," she said, a touch of laughter in her voice. If he had understood such things better he may have detected a little world-worn cynicism in that laughter too, but emotions… well, they were hard. So to him it was just a joyous little chuckle.

"It moves," he said, finally finding his voice again and snatching a glance back at the clock face as he did so.

"What now?" Jolene asked, a look of confusion crossing her face. That was an emotion he knew well enough as he saw it in the mirror more often than not.

"The hands, they move," he explained, or tried to do so, pointing up at the clock face.

"Of course they do, hun, that's what clock hands do," she said, her voice holding the confusion now, though there was a touch of pity to her tone too. He had come to recognise pity as well. It was an emotion he found he inspired in others quite often when he said things that confused them.

He was not sure he liked pity, or inspiring it in others at any rate…

Frowning now, he just nodded towards her, shrugged his shoulders and turned back to his mop. Trying to put that moment of pity out of his mind, he set off mopping, once more chasing the rainbows into the floor. But as he did so he found he was thinking of Jolene's cherry red smile, and in thinking of that he found his own once more…

"I swear that man is queerer than a six nickel note at times!" Jolene muttered, half to herself, as she watched the grey man waltz on with his mop and bucket.

"There's no malice in him, dearest," a voice said from behind her. A voice she knew well, as she had heard it in her head for the longest time. Yet, she realised, the voice sounded strange right then, though the why of it was not something she could not put her finger on.

"Oh, I know there ain't, man's as goodhearted as they come, but that don't stop him being a loon. Which I guess makes him no worse than all of em and no better, come to that," Jolene said with a sighing lilt.

"He has more excuse than most of them, dearest," the voice said, somewhat archly, and Jolene turned towards its owner, looking down towards the floor. Which left her feeling oddly perturbed to find herself staring down at a pair of kitten-heels, and having to raise her gaze to meet their owner's eyes.

"Oh…" Jolene said. And it was then she realised what had been strange about the voice was simply that she had heard it.

The woman stood before her, who was not really called Bringer of Things, looked quizzically back at Jolene for a moment, then smiled briefly, registering Jolene's confusion, and shifted in a strange way so she was no longer standing on two feet but four. Jolene's gaze dropped down once more and met with eyes like pools of darkness flecked with green.

"Sorry, dearest one, I did not intend to surprise you," said the cat, with a voice Jolene heard inside her head.

Jolene in turn found herself glancing furtively between the cat and the piano player, then back. A number of little tumblers clicked into place at the back of her mind and with them came a strange wave of sadness tinged with joy.

"Oh hunny, oh my..." she managed. "I suspected but..."

If a cat could manage to look both amused and apologetic at the same time then that was the expression that met Jolene's words of sympathy.

"So, I was right, you're... You were... Oh my," she said, still a little shaken by the idea.

The cat turned to look towards the piano a moment then turned back to Jolene and nodded ever so slightly. "I was, for a little while, but no more," the cat said with a tinge of remorse. "Till death do us... as the saying goes..."

"Oh my," Jolene managed again, feeling tears welling up behind her eyes and damning her own sentimentality, which she felt was cursed to be the death of her mascara.

The cat tilted its head to the left and made a face

that could not possibly be one of regret, but was all the same. "He will be able to move on now, that is all that matters," the cat said, but Jolene wondered if that was true. She was far from sure the cat truly understood the grief Jolene saw in the Piano Player's eyes whenever he spoke about his wife's death. Even if the cat who was no more a cat than she had been a woman moments earlier, and if she was truly what Jolene had for a long time suspected… 'Well,' Jolene thought, 'how does the divine understand mortality? How could it even hope to…?'

"I pray you're right…" Jolene found herself saying after a moment, far from convinced, and not entirely conscious of her choice of words.

"I'm sure I will be, there is another who'll take my place in his heart…" the cat said, with the strange certainness Jolene had come to consider more like pronouncements of what was to be, rather than conjecture on the feline's part.

For a fleeting second Jolene wondered if this had been some form of hint, and she gave the Piano Player a glance, before shaking her head and dismissing the idea, she had no such feelings towards Richard. Oh, he was pleasant enough, but quite aside anything else he was twenty years her junior and truth told Jolene had always preferred men of a certain vintage. The cat must have seen her glance all the same, for with some rye amusement it continued… "Not you, dearest one, don't worry I'm not playing the match maker. Besides you have your own romantic entanglements ahead I think without you being involved in mine…"

"Really now, I'm sure that is the most ridiculous thing I've heard all day…" Jolene laughed, with only a touch of bitterness at the suggestion, barring a lifelong infatuation for a certain singer with killer sideburns she had long since put romantic notions aside.

The cat, in a way that no cat could, motioned towards the receding Greyman, now well beyond the pool table, mopping corners of the bar that dared not speak their name.

"Now y'all being ridiculous..." Jolene said. Though she found her gaze, having followed the cat's nod towards the man in grey with the small yellow smiley badge in his lapel, lingering there a moment longer than strictly necessary...

"Do you mind if I change back?" the cat asked and in doing so put a spur in Jolene's chain of thought.

"Of course not, hunny..." Jolene replied, finding herself still a little distracted by the way Greyman was moving in the corners, something about the way his hips swayed a little as he danced along to the music. Something he was unconscious of she was sure, but it reminded her of a young singer she had first seen on the Ed Sullivan show in her youth. The comparison struck her with a wave of mild embarrassment, so she turned away and back to the cat, who was no longer a cat, and was back in kitten-heels.

"Thank you kindly, dearest one. The trouble with morphic resonance is once you decide on a shape for the day you really need to stick with it if you don't want to bring on an ungodly headache..." the woman in kitten-heels said.

"Oh, I know what you mean," Jolene said, nodding, though she didn't.

"Now, weren't we talking about romantic entanglements?" the woman said with a very cat like smile, and a hint of feline humour...

"I'm quite certain we'd dropped that subject," Jolene replied, fighting an urge to turn her gaze once more in the direction of the far corner of the barroom. She felt flustered all of a sudden and found, somewhat unexpectedly, she was entirely sure why.

"As you wish, dearest, but if I was you I'd ask him about clocks again sometime, he has a story to tell about them, I'm sure..." the woman in kitten-heels said slyly.

Jolene tried to hide a wave of embarrassment behind a laugh of mock derision. "You think everyone has a story to tell, missy," she ventured.

"That's only because they do, Jolene, haven't you realised that yet...?"

Jolene narrowed her eyes a moment, but then found herself smiling once more. Somehow the woman in kitten-heels always managed to make her smile, even when she wasn't wearing heels.

"I'm sure you're right, but anyway I must get on," Jolene said and turned on her own heels, which were of a more sensible variety as favoured by waitresses who spend all day on their feet the world over, and headed off towards the kitchen, pausing only so slightly to look towards the far corner of the bar and the man dancing with his mop once more on the way. It was only as she reached for the kitchen door that another thought occurred to her and she turned back to the woman in kitten-heels.

"Where do the clothes go? Or come from? Whatever, you know what I mean..." she asked her, and witnessed a sly, not entirely un-feline, smile, pass across the woman's face.

"Well, I'm sure I'd cause quite a scene if I was naked, dearest. Doubtless there are one or two customers that might appreciate that kind of thing, but we're not running a strip joint just yet, are we…?" the woman in kitten-heels replied.

"Yes, but where do they go when you, you know?" Jolene asked, seriously intrigued all of a sudden. She tried miming shrinking to cat size and back with her hands, in case her question was unclear, which she did with an eloquence doomed to look just a little ridiculous.

"A woman becomes a cat, then the cat becomes a woman once more and your question is where does she get the clothes?" came an amused reply.

"Well, yes…" Jolene said, with a touch of a huff to her voice, she was sure now she was been made fun of, which struck her as unfair.

The woman smiled a sly little smile and replied with a lilt of laughter to her voice. "Well, it's all a matter of perception, my dearest one. I'm not really wearing anything… What are clothes, when it all comes down to it, if not another kind of skin after all?"

Jolene blushed, rather more so than a woman of a certain age likes to blush, and decided to bid a hasty retreat back to the kitchen. Suspecting there was still a little of the mischief of a kitten in the woman who was no longer a cat. Still somewhat peeved as she stepped through the hatchway doors, she muttered rather too loudly to herself, "It, must be those darn kitten-heels…"

"What's that?" the chef asked, looking up from a particularly difficult sea bass table four was going to order in ten minutes' time.

"The cat… She's… Oh, she's just being herself as usual…" Jolene snapped back with more venom than she intended, which just added to the irritation. Feeling a little overwhelmed by the whole conversation, she stormed straight though the kitchen and out into the garden to talk to Morn.

"What cat?" the chef inquired of her departing thunder. Then shrugged to himself and went back to fileting…

"The clock in the station always said 8:15 when I arrived," Greyman told her. He was sitting on a barstool, leaning on the bar itself. Cradling a 'Sex on the Beach' with a slice of orange and a pink cocktail umbrella in the top.

It was so late it was early and he and Jolene were sitting together at the corner of the bar where it turned back into the wall.

Jolene had suggested they have a drink together when the bar closed.

In return Greyman had explained, with mild confusion on his part, that he didn't "know yet if I will be thirsty."

To this reply, an expression had crossed Jolene's face he had since come to recognise meant he had said the wrong thing.

A few days later when she had calmed down enough to suggest they have a drink after work again, he was more prepared and told her, "I will make sure I'm thirsty."

The expression this inspired he could not read at all, but he was surprised when having avoiding drinking anything for the rest of the day, he had found himself sitting alone in the bar that night.

A few days later Greyman had discussed these strange events with Richard and the piano player had pointed out to him that, "Jolene doesn't care if you want a drink or not, she just wants to spend some time in your company alone," and added that if he wanted to do the same he should, "be the one who asks her this time," as he had "royally screwed up" when she'd asked him.

After considering what Richard had told him, Greyman had later cornered Jolene by the serving hatch and asked her, "Are you likely to be thirsty after the bar closes this evening?"

A day later, armed with more advice from Richard, as well as from Morn, Sonny, she who was not a cat at the moment, and even Lyal (whose advice was a little too literal), Greyman waited by the serving hatch again and when Jolene tried to pass, he pulled out the piece of paper upon which he had written down exactly what they had all told him to say.

"Jolene," he read out to her, "would you like to have a drink at the bar with me tonight, as I would very much like to do so whether or not either of us is thirsty, because the drink and the thirst is not the important thing, it's the company that matters and I would like to share a hour or two with you?"

Despite being one of the longest sentences Greyman had ever spoken, and the momentary look that crossed the waitress's face which suggested he had not quite got it right yet again, he had been somewhat relieved when she smiled and agreed to meeting him for a drink that night…

Which was where the subject of clocks was brought

up again. Hence the story he had begun to tell, and while you could not have blamed Jolene for glazing over a little due to Greyman's somewhat monotone delivery, surprisingly she was listening with almost morbid fascination. Though she did find herself momentarily pondering if this was a case of being a rabbit in the headlights, so to speak.

"Sometimes I was early, sometimes I was late. But the clock always said quarter past eight," he told her.

"Did you rhyme that on purpose?" Jolene asked, all innocent humour behind her cherry red smile. He found himself wondering if she was mocking him. Then realised to his surprise he did not care if she was, as long as she continued smiling in his direction.

He shook his head and continued, "The train couldn't ever be late, you see. The ministry insisted they run on time. It's a well-known sign of an efficient bureaucracy, you see, that the trains run on time."

"I thought that was fascism?" his drinking partner inquired before taking a sip of Bud. She having opted for a plain beer over the kind of luminous cocktails Greyman favoured.

"I don't follow?"

"Mussolini, bald Italian guy, famous for jack boots and getting the trains to run one time?"

"I don't think I've heard of him," he said, bemused.

"That's okay, hunny, the short-arse ain't worth the time it would take to explain. Go on with your story," she told him with a certain amount of feeling.

He looked at her for a moment, feeling slightly intoxicated, not by the drink but by her eyes, which were still hazel, which seemed the most wonderful of colours. He took a sip of his cocktail and continued.

"The trains were always on time because the hands on the clock never moved, you see. It was always 8:15 no matter how early or late I got to the station."

"You mean, the clock didn't tell time?" she asked.

"No, it told time. It was just always the same time, that way the trains were never late."

"Oh, so the clock in the station always read 8:15 and the trains all arrived at 8:15 so they could claim they were never late?" she asked, though he was not sure she really understood.

"No, not claim they were never late, because they were never late, they couldn't be because the clock was always right," he tried to explain. "Because the ministry said the clock was right, and if the ministry say a thing then that thing is true, imperially."

"Right, okay but that's not actually true is it, I mean just because the clock in the station says 8:15 doesn't mean the train turns up at 8:15, does it? It's just a clock, it's not, you know, actual time," Jolene said, looking frustrated by the logic that was obvious to him, but he realised suddenly the cause of the misunderstanding.

"Sorry, I see how I've confused you. I'm not explaining this well at all. You see the trains don't turn up at 8:15 at all, the trains turn up at 8:20," he said, which caused her to erupt in laughter that confused him once more, which the look on his face made evident he suspected, since she raised a hand of apology and tried to stifle her laughter. Taking a swig of her beer as much to gather her thoughts, he suspected, she took a moment then tried to work through the logic without bursting into laughter again.

"So, let me see if I have this right. The trains never turn up late? You all pile in the station at 8:15, because that's what the time it says on the clock. And, as it's 8:15 according to the clock, the train is never late because the train can't arrive till it's 8:20? So you all just stand there waiting for trains that never come, but are never late?" she said, failing to keep little bursts of laughter from slipping out between her cherry red lips.

Greyman felt frustrated, which was not uncommon when he tried to explain aspects of his former life to those who worked in the Passing Place, but with Jolene in particular he wanted her to understand. Though he could not have explained to anyone why that was the case. So he took a moment to explain the last bit of information which she was missing.

"No, I missed a bit, sorry, the trains came at 8:20, they always arrived at 8:20, because when they arrived the men with the stepladders would come out and move the clock hands, so the train was on time."

Jolene erupted in delighted laugher.

It was a laugh full of joy, a laugh full of colour. A laugh Greyman found as strange and wonderful as colour itself.

Then she put down her beer, leaned towards him, much to his surprise, put her arms around him and kissed him.

Her cherry red lips on his.

It was at this moment, Greyman realised there were thing ever stranger and more wonderful than colour…

And found himself kissing her back.

Authors note

I would not normally add a note to a short story, but this is an exception. The events in this story take place after those in the novel Passing Place. Both Greyman and Jolene are relatively minor characters in that novel, but like all the characters in that novel they live in my imagination and have their own stories I've never written down. Which is what happens when you spend five years with a bunch of characters while you write a novel which is mostly about one of them. Also, the cat told me to write this, and I wasn't going to argue. Only a fool argues with the cat.

A MESSAGE FROM THE SATIMONIOUS ORDER OF THE WILLING SACRIFICE

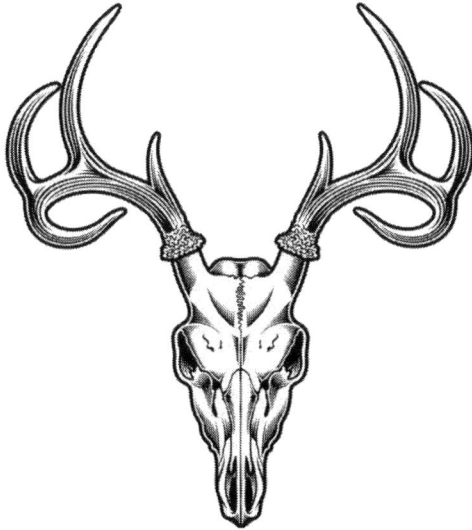

We, The Sanctimonious Order of the Willing Sacrifice, must regrettably start this annual meeting by apologising, but once again, for the tenth year running, we have failed to secure a year king.

While there are of course be those who scoff at what some claim are our 'out dated religious observances' we feel obliged to point out that it is our belief the willing sacrifice of a year king at Yule has been bringing forth bounteous years of fortune, good weather, and good health for the people of Albion for thousands of years. It is our belief, therefore, that it is the dearth of Year kings, of which there have only been two this century, is the cause of recent hardships.

Extreme weather, floods, so called 'climate change', pandemics, wildfires, the steady decline of decent script writing in recent seasons of doctor who, Boris Johnson, the continued lack of spangles, can all be attributed to the lack of a viable and willing sacrifice at the Yule celebrations. Frankly the selfishness of people never ceases to astound us, and that the sun continues to be renewed for the coming year we can only put down to stubbornness on the part of Hydrogen.

Why no bright and handsome youth is willing to become the new year king each Yule we can only conclude is due to a general lack of moral foundation among the youth of today.

We are willing to except that there has also been something of a lack of bountiful bevies of buxom maidens willing to give up a year of their lives to serve as hand maidens to a year king. This we believe is because they all seem to prefer to spend a gap year in Thailand or Australia, having a wild time and engaging in the excessive hedonism of some of the so-called eastern religions. Rather than feeding grapes to a numbskull pretty boy in a smokey round house. This is also regrettable.

There is also the unfortunate matter of the round house been caught up in the Thatcherism of the early 80's and us been forced to sell it off as technically it was a council owned tenement. But we have procured a small flat above a chinses takeaway in Salisbury for the use of the Year King. We will admit it is a little under repaired, pokey, and if you dislike the smell of boiled rice you may need a good air freshener, but many would think it was an improvement on a wattle and daub round house with no central heating. Though the flat only has a three-bar electric fire and only two of the bars work.

The bounteous feast of fruit, meats and ale is still there for the year king of course. Admittedly due to fiscal constraints, through the day these are limited to a 'meal deal' from the local Tesco's. Which is also why we generally can only supply 2 litre bottles of white lightening cider. But the thought is there and there is a duck at Easter, well Peking duck if you order the two for one special at Mr Hong's downstairs.

But all this aside we still believe we offer a fabulous, one year only, limited time experience, for the volunteer year king, and Sharon who works in the chippy, while getting on in years, is still willing to peal grapes on a Wednesday afternoon, and wear the traditional ox skin loin coverings and nothing else… on warm summer days at least, the rest of the year she insists on wearing a dressing gown, but as she is the far side of seventy now and so we feel this may be a blessing to all.

She does however make a really good sweet-nettle tea.

We are aware there has been some disgruntlement in the order this year, with suggestions from Mr Wallaby that given the continuing decline of the environment, and the way mars bars as smaller than they used to be, we should perhaps look into the possibility of an 'unwilling' sacrifice this year. Even going so far as to suggest 'that Jones lad from two doors down, who broken my gnome with his football last month.'

We will state once again, an unwilling sacrifice does not placate the ancient ones. They also are a lot more work. They always squirm about on the alter, and that makes it difficult to cut out there still beating heart cleanly, and the authorities look down on that kind of thing.

It makes a right mess on the rug

Any who, I will end this missive here. If anyone knows of a likely lad willing to be a year king tell them to drop us a line at PO Box 1010, Dudley Salterton. Also, even if we cannot find a year king, bountiful bevies of buxom maidens are still also required, and given these days of equality a year queen, or indeed a year Queenking, or Kingqueen would we think be just as acceptable...

Yours...
Earnest Wilberforce,
Arch Druid
The Sanctimonious Order of the Willing Sacrifice
Royal Air Force, Retired.

TWENTY-SEVEN

27

I was born on the 3rd of December 1833. I'd been aware of my existence for two months prior to my painful disturbing entry into the world, or for twenty-seven years, depending how you look at it.

It was on that early December morning I learned first-hand what a blessing it had been that I had no recollection of my previous birth. For I shall tell you this much, humans were never meant to be truly self-aware when we are born. Our births are traumatic enough for our mothers, traumatic enough for ourselves, without us being fully conscious of being pushed into the world.

You're confused, I know. You'll think me mad, and in truth there have been many occasions I have doubted my own sanity. But the 3rd of December 1833 was not my first birth and two months before that day, I died.

It was, as I remember, a particularly painful prolonged death. They had plied me with morphine but just enough to stop my screaming. It would have been a kindness for them to cut short my suffering with a blade to the throat, or to have smothered me with a pillow. Instead, they let me linger for days in silent agony from the fateful sabre wound that had near disembowelled me.

There was no solace to be had in that wound. It was not a wound taken in honour. I had been gutted in a pointless duel over an ill-advised insult, an insult I had given. I'd been drunk at the time, heady with perceived success. I'd been celebrating what I foolishly considered to be my artful seduction of a senior officer's wife.

In that life I was a cavalry man. In truth, no more than a lowly second lieutenant, but full of myself as such men so often are, without any real achievements to my name. That night, I was regaling my fellows in the regimental mess with the tale of my amorous adventures with an artillery major's wife. As I told it, to the hilarity of all, I believed, she was a woman with a firm little arse but a face only the blind would call pretty. I went further, as the laughter grew, making some off-colour remarks. You know the kind of thing.

Before you judge me, know only that I was a different person then. Literally in fact. In later lives I would come to hate the kind of man I had been. The kind of man who would say something like, "You don't look at the mantle while you're poking the fire."

Unfortunately, the man I was then was obliviously unaware the woman in question was the sister of a captain in my regiment. A captain sat but a table away from me and my rowdy compatriots, as I took things even further, profanely acting out of my amorous adventures for the benefit of my friends. If my 'friends' that night knew the captain was the lady's sibling, they did nothing to rein in my coarseness, nor did they warn me he had risen to his feet behind me, doubtless enraged. If they had, I suspect I would not have proclaimed that we should call her 'the regimental horse,' as not only I, but so many of my fellow officers in the King's 9th had taken a ride astride her.

That there was some truth in this does not lessen my guilt. Lady Gertrude had a thing for young horsemen, and a husband with no interest in her save her money. But while I was not alone in my conquest of the major's wife, I was the first man stupid enough to brag about doing so in the mess, in her brother's presence.

So it was I came by my pointless death in a pointless duel with Captain Hans Fredrick. A duel I agreed to flushed with youthful arrogance, an inflated sense of my own abilities, and a stomach full of wine. I wish I could claim it became a famous duel, epic in proportion, fought between two master swordsman. I wish I could say that we fenced for hours, that it was ill-luck that caused the misstep that cost me my life. In truth, he knocked aside my sabre with ease and gutted me with a simple riposte. I remember clearly as he stood over me, his earlier rage giving way to disgust. He spat upon me as I lay in agony on a grassy lawn and walked away without giving me a second glance.

My cohorts dragged me to the infirmary, those bosom friends of mine. Dragged me through the doors and dumped me in a cot to die. Then doubtless returned to their drinks and perhaps a hand of cards. In the week it took me to die, not one of them visited me again. I dare say they knew my worth. I can't say I blame them.

The surgeon patched me up, but gangrene set in on the second day. Eating away at me from the inside. A slow painful ignominious death for 2nd lieutenant Arthur Maydew. A bitter end to a pointless unremarkable life. I would not have believed it at the time, but now I look back on Arthur's life I doubt even his father was much moved at the funeral of his third and most disappointing son. I wasn't there of course. Well, no more than anyone attends their own funeral. I was there in body, my spirit though had already moved on. I suspect it was a pathetic little gathering. Few tears shed by the few bothering to attend. But I doubt it matters, as I say,

I was already elsewhere. Though nowhere anyone expects to find themselves after a painful slow death finally drags you to your end, saving the Buddhists and Hindus of this world. But even they do not expect to plunge from the agony of a gangrenous death straight into the dark smothering warmth of the womb, least ways not fully conscious of the life they have just so bitterly departed.

Sigmund Freud made much of the sanctuary of the womb. He would have it that we long to return to the safety and security that our subconscious remembers feeling as each of us floated in the darkness and warmth of utero. He would have it that we recall, deep within, a sense of wellbeing we can never recapture. That we long once again to feel the vibration and sound of our mother's heartbeat. It is because of this unconscious desire that we strive to return to such a state all our lives, driven by our very id to seek the impossible and recapture that nirvana that was the precious bond we felt with our mothers within the womb.

Sigmund was wrong, trust me on this, because having returned to the womb, believe me, nothing is quite so terrifying.

The moment of Arthur's passing, I passed into the blind half formed foetus that would house my next existence. In that realm of total sensory deprivation, I was overwhelmed by heat and vibrations. The dull resonant thud of my mother's heartbeat encompassed everything and it felt akin to drowning. You can trust me on that too… There is nothing reassuring about being in utero. Floating in utter darkness, at the mercy of the unknown, utterly helpless and utterly alone.

That said, being in utero is probably more reassuring if you're not self-aware. If you lack the recollection of departing the mortal coil in agony moments before. Added to which I knew I had led a less than saintly life. Combined with the knowledge of my own death, I remember feeling I was in some cruel purgatory that first time. I knew not what was happening to me. I was in the dark, both figuratively and literally. But I knew as Arthur Maydew I hadn't led an exemplary life.

Arthur had been raised in the Anglican tradition but he little cared for the church's doctoring of abstinence and good Christian values. The third son of a respectable family he'd wasted what few talents he'd been gifted on a string of pointless endeavours. When other avenues for advancement had been used up, he'd talked his father into funding a commission with horse guards. And why was that? Did he, the I that was, have some driving patriotic compulsion to serve his country? No, it was simply because he fancied himself in the uniform.

I was, not to put too fine a point on it, a drunken lout, a womaniser and a bully. I was a man who delighted in abusing what little power I possessed. The kind of officer who punishes the men under his command for the slightest infraction, perceived or real. I took pleasure handing out the worst punishments I could design and then took even more pleasure in bragging about it afterwards. In short, I was something of a shit and I knew it too. So, when I found myself floating in the darkness and heat of utero after my timely demise, well, I was convinced I was in hell. A hell I richly deserved.

And then, on the 3rd of December, I was born

again, in the literal not religious sense.

That too led to its own strange purgatory.

To say I was a strange infant is an understatement. I was strange in that I knew who and what I was. Yet I was still an infant, with an infant's control over my bladder, an infant's control over my emotions, and an infant's ability to communicate those emotions. I was in fact as helpless as any other infant despite being aware of my previous life, I was also no more able to understand my mother's words than any other infant. My body was new for all my soul was old. I could not understand why this was but in time I came to understand a little about the chemistry of the brain. Neurons need to make the connections before what you hear becomes something you can understand. The same applies to speech and any other aspect of the physical. If anything, knowledge of my prior existence only made my new one harder.

My mother tried, like any mother, to calm her infant, but I screamed, flailed and struggled all the more.

In time, this new me was christened Brian Caine and I came to answer to that name. The memories of Arthur and aspects of his life became clouded like an adult's memories of childhood. Despite those memories, I had to relearn so much. Maths, science, language were concepts I learned anew. What I remembered of such things from my former life were broken echoes of another's past. In this new life I was a son of paupers, who I came to resent far more than their due. As Brian, I was put to work in a mill age six and schooled on Sundays with Methodist redemption between the alphabet and numbers. Those early years in the mills were hard and bred a bitterness within me born of Arthur. I had memories of an earlier life of privilege. I remembered too well the joys and arrogance of wealth. I came to believe the hardships of Brian's life were God's punishment for Arthur's misdeeds, but rather than being pushed by this towards piousness, I took the other road. Resentment, anger, bitterness… this was my creed. When of an age I took to drink, and with it, thievery. In a short time, Brian came to have even less to recommend him than Arthur. Perhaps that speaks to my character, that given a second turn of the wheel, I came out all the worse. As Brian grew older, so his crimes grew, and his bitterness with it. Eventually such a life will always catch a man up and in time it did. A drunken fight over a few shillings ended with a blade in the gut, another this time, not my own. But for that blade I was brought up before the beak, and the blade proved the death of me as surely as if it had been stuck in me. The man in the wig sentenced me to the gallows before the sunset on that day, the day after I had just turned twenty-seven for the second time.

The irony did nothing to sooth my bitterness, but as I walked to the gallows it occurred to me that was almost to the day the same age as Arthur had been when he lost his fateful duel. I remember making some acrimonious remark to the hangman, "Better luck in the next one then…" Of course, I had not known, I had not realised the truth of my existence, not then, as the trapdoor fell away and I dropped to Brian's doom as the rope around his neck snapped tight.

Twenty-seven… Years after Brian, Jimi Hendrix was to die at twenty-seven and so did Janice Joplin. They weren't alone. Jim Morrison, Brian Jones, Amy

Whitehouse, Kurt Cobain. Not to mention Robert Johnson, the father of the blues, who sold his soul to the devil at the crossroads. All dead at twenty-seven. Like Arthur, like Brian… There's something about that age, it's not just musicians that die at that age. Racing drivers, sportsmen, poets, kings, emperors… even popes. Three of them in fact, though the one that stands out is John XII, the pope who turned the Vatican into a brothel and died ignominiously in bed with a married woman from a fatal stroke. God's judgement on his wayward priest some might say… How do I know this odd piece of trivia? Well, maybe I'm a little obsessed with the number twenty-seven, but then I was that age when gangrene took my life as Arthur and twenty-seven again in 1860 when as Brian I walked to the hangman's noose.

Seventeen years later in 1877, Richard Thwaite, a cobbler's son, left Doncaster and joined the army to avoid a life of nailing boots. Ten years passed and he'd done well, raised through the ranks to the giddy hights of sergeant. Richard was a pious man. He swore off strong drink, though he remembered the taste of ale and the joys of drunkenness from his other lives. He was well liked, though some thought him too soft on the men for a sergeant. But he was good at it, he remembered soldiering, all be it from astride horse and as a life it suited Richard. He was asked once by an officer why he was so forgiving of his men. He told the officer he was trying to be a better man, to make up for his past. Which was true, but not in a way the officer would ever have believed.

One hand on his rifle, and one hand on his bible, Richard Thwaite marched to the army's drum and tried to guide rough angry drunken louts to a better path. He felt he was doing the Lord's work as well as the Queen's, and he hoped in doing so he might break his curse. For he had become convinced this third life was his chance to rectify the black stains upon his soul that Arthur and Brian's lives had left...

Then just before he turned twenty-seven Richard, or rather I, was posted to Zululand as a new colony was founded. I thought little of it, the war was done, it was a peaceful little backwater. A few weeks later, not long after the anniversary of my third birth, there under a foreign sun, the regiment celebrated Queen Victoria's golden jubilee. I remember being happy, drinking tea while others drank to the Queen's health with stronger beverages, laughing with friends as the men fired off their rifles in salute to Her Majesty. I was still laughing at the drunk antics of the men when the bullet hit me.

It was an ignominious death all told. An accident. What odds would you lay a stray air-shot would whistle down and punch through heart and lung. Killing Richard dead in an instant. Killing me without giving me even a moment to regret my passing...

Back I went to the womb, that all too familiar purgatory. Floating in utero, with the memories of three lives and a number for company...

So, you'll forgive me if I became obsessed with the number twenty-seven when next I was born two months later in Calcutta. Born daughter of a house maid working for a British family. That then was a shock. First I saw my mother's light brown face, and then more so when I realised what was not between my legs.

That mother of mine came from Buddhist stock,

rare but not unheard of in that part of India. She taught me her beliefs as she raised me, unaware that I had my own strange perspective upon them. She helped me though and as Brinda I came to terms a little with the oddity of my existence. Though life as an Indian girl in Calcutta at the turn of the century was complicated enough. More so for I remember lives as a man, and I was who I was. That I found hardest to reconcile, my predilection had not changed, and in those days, a woman attracted only to women was something the world did not accept. I fled India to avoid a marriage I did not want and became a nurse in a country I knew better than any would believe and hid who I was as best I could. But of my other lives and that damn number, I was reconciled by 1914 and when the war came, I volunteered to serve as a nurse behind the front lines. The Great War as we were calling it then. I knew what would be coming, as Brinda had reconciled with my fate. I almost welcomed her coming end, while I sought to ease the suffering of others and seek some karmic balance to my strange existence. All the stranger having lived a life as a her.

Though if Buddhism help me reconcile to my fate, I was not so reconciled I did not feel terror the night the shells started to fall.

Twenty-seven years later, a midshipman named Alec was feeling a growing sense of dread as he stood upon a Hawaiian beach. Another life, a different nationality, a different service, but I knew something was coming as my birthday slipped past. Perhaps I could have warned them, but who would have listened to my warnings. Alec's was a difficult life, growing up through the great depression. Son of an evangelist pastor, brought up on God and redemption, and believing in neither. Christ had no answers, nothing in the Bible explained my plight, and my father's belt was the only answer to any question I asked of him.

To escape the tyranny of a pious man and the poverty of the dust bowl, I'd joined the navy to see the world once more. I did well, as I always did, I'd come to like the military life. I was marked as a man who showed no fear, but it's easy not to fear when you know at twenty it's not your time to die. Though my fellow sailors found me strange at times when it came to talk of women. Not for me a leering glance or whistle as a girl walked past. I'd led a life on the other side of such things. A life that had given me a new perspective all around. I tried to treat each the same, no matter what hung, or not, between their legs, or the colour of their skin. But as twenty-seven came around in 1941, I wondered if Alec had made a difference in the lives of anyone, as I stood upon that beach, a little place called Pearl Harbour, and watched the zeros flying in. Well, I'm sure you can guess the rest.

Twenty-seven years later, it was the swinging sixties. Julie Sunburst, another sapphic life, but so different this time round. Julie burned her bra and freaked out to The Beatles and The Stones. I knew too well what would come at twenty-seven. I was doomed to die… Again, and again as that number rolled around. But there is a freedom in such a fate. I took risks, took drugs, and lived the wild child life. I was the queen of free love, the epitome of a flower child. I taught eastern spiritualism and the love of life to hippies and freaks in Frisco. The life of a woman in the sixties was freer than it had ever been. Freer than an Indian girl's at the turn of the century. And the drugs, oh the drugs. The wonder of LSD. I overdosed twice in 66 but wow what a trip that was. They called me wild, and wild I was…

But then…

Maybe it was a side effect of all the drugs, a hangover long overdue. Maybe I was just burnt out, too many lives lived, too many times rebooted… As the year turned in 68, a strange depression took hold of me. I came to believe in my soul that I wanted it all to end. I wanted to be done with my endless prolonged existence. I had no wish to face another life, to take another throw of the dice, another turn of the wheel. I got it in my head to end it all, to have an end so absolute that there could be no coming back this time. I hitched my way to Nevada, to join the protests outside of the boxcar tests.

Make love not war…

I chose a third way, I chose oblivion, and stole across the fences. I ran across the desert to embrace the bomb. To embrace that most unholy creation of the atomic age. I wanted an end to it all, an end of me. I wanted, no, needed, a final death, I sought it out. A final end to my prolonged existence beneath the mushroom cloud…

Nineteen-ninety-five and as a man, I was still alive.

Sarajevo, another battlefield, another war. Mankind never learns and neither do I. It had come to me that humans are fated to keep repeating their mistakes, one generation to the next. The 60s gave me hope that the cycle might end, for all I ended them in despair. That was the generation who could have changed it all, so what the hell happened to them as they grew old. It made me thankful I never had. This time I'd been born in England once more, too late for punk, though I knew their rage. Thatcher's children sickened me, putting money put ahead of common decency.

I joined the army once again, guess I don't learn either, but it's what I knew best. When in 95, twenty-seven rolled round once more, and I died to not one bullet but a score. Protecting a child, my body his shield. I hope he lived and the wounds of war would heal. I wondered then if sacrifice was the key, if my life for another's would set me free...

Which brings me to here, as I sit in this bar, talking to you. This latest life was much like the last. Now it's all but done with, all but the shouting. What have I learnt, over all these lives? I remember them all Arthur, Brian, Richard, Brinda, Alec, Sunbeam Starburst as Julie was known, Frankie the one who saved the life of a child and me, finally me, till the next one comes around. Yet I've nothing to share for all those lives, all those faiths. It's all still a mystery to me. And why twenty-seven? Who the hell knows. Ask Jimmy and Janis if you meet them, if they're still around.

I've sought out others, you see, over the years. Sought people like me, living life after life. I found only frauds, hoodwinks and fools. So maybe we all follow the same path, maybe the souls of all of us come back. But if that's true then I've seen no proof of others and know only my own. So maybe it's just me or maybe us all, but if you're banking on answers, well, I have them not.

It's 2022 and it's been, well, a strange couple of years. I didn't fear the pandemic, not yet at least, but my birthday is coming and orders have arrived. Another war, another conflict, another opportunity to die. Another chance this might end, but I suspect it will not. Twenty-seven will destine me to the womb once again.

So, what have I learnt?

What do I know?

What advice can I give you, some great insight before I go?

Life's short, you should live it… unlike me, you may not get another go.

PIROTHERAPY

"It's not that I always wanted to be a pirate, you understand. I mean, when I was ten, I wanted to be a ninja. Ninjas were cool, you know? Dressed in black, hiding in the shadows, throwing out those steel death stars…" I said, wistfully, leaning against the back of the boat, my arm resting lazily over the rudder.

"Shuriken," my companion commented, in what I felt was a deliberately annoying Bavarian accent. Some might consider this unreasonable of me given he was after all German. Well, if we are being exact, Austrian, but accent-wise there is little difference to the Anglo-Saxon ear. The thing was, however, I was sure he was deliberately making his accent more pronounced than normal because he was speaking English to demonstrate some abstract point. But regardless I replied…

"What?"

"Shuriken. It's the correct Japanese name for those 'ninja throwing stars' as you referred to them," he explained, taking no small joy in doing so. He was always a man who liked to explain things in order to demonstrate his superior knowledge.

"So? What does that matter? God's sake, why do you have to be such a pedant?" I bemoaned, which might have been a tad over-dramatic as reactions go, but when the circumstances you find yourself in involve finding yourself cast adrift in an open boat, with nothing but ocean on the horizon, it can make you a little testy.

"One would have thought if one wished to be a ninja one would have the wherewithal to learn the correct name for 'ninja throwing stars'…" he expanded, in a calm, reasonable and damn annoying voice.

"I was ten!" I retorted. "Who knows the right name

for anything when they're ten?"

"When I was a boy one would always make sure to look everything up in one's encyclopaedia…" my companion further explained, pausing to stroke his beard and narrowing his eyes, clearly intending to expand even further still on his impromptu lecture.

I narrowed my own eyes in return. "Yes… I'm sure you did, but I was talking about normal children…"

He let out a pompous little laugh, more a snort than anything. "Oh, I'm sure all normal children want to be shinobi spies and assassins when they are ten years old," he condescended. He was remarkably good at being condescending, but all considered I don't suppose that's much of a surprise.

"Shin… What?"

"Shinobi. It's the correct Japanese term for ninjas. 'Ninja' is a low term, slang as it were. Indeed, it was in nature something of an insult, though being Japanese it is a very stylised insult…" he said, pausing to clean salt spray off his glasses.

"For the love of god, how is any of that relevant?" I asked him.

"That is an interesting question, is it not, but then you were about to tell me why you wanted to be a pirate, but then, for some reason, you brought up ninjas." He returned his spectacles to their accustomed position, so he could look inquiringly at me over the rims.

"I was illustrating a point," I said, trying to keep my frustration out of my voice.

"I see, and the point you were illustrating would be?"

"That I didn't always want to be a pirate," I explained.

"I see..." was his only response.

"What do you mean 'I see'?"

"I comprehend, I understand, I grasp, I..."

"Okay, okay, I get it. But anyway, the point I was trying to make was I didn't always want to be a pirate. For a while I wanted to be a ninja..."

"Shinobi..."

"Whatever. After ninja I remember wanting to be a cowboy for a while, then there was my astronaut phase, then Spider-Man..."

"Spiderman? You wanted to be half man half spider?" he inquired, peering at me once more.

"Yes... I mean no.... I mean I wanted to be Spider-Man, you know, Spider-Man, the superhero."

"A super, hero?"

"How can you know so much about the Japanese names for ninjas and throwing stars, yet not what a superhero is?" I asked with genuine surprise.

"I'm unfamiliar with the concept. It is perhaps the burden of one's existence to know many things but not know many others. Unless of course this is something that came along after my time?"

"Oh... yer, I guess that make sense. They are more a twentieth century thing, you're more nineteenth, ain't you?" I said, as I realised that the strangest thing about finding myself dressed as a pirate and adrift on a seemingly endless ocean in an open boat, was not the boat, the ocean or the battered tricorn hat I was wearing, but the company I'd found myself in.

"Not really. I lived a full life that spanned both centuries," the famous Doctor of Psychology stated.

"Well yes, but you died in the nineteen thirties," I said, reasonably sure of myself on this fact as I had spent some time studying him in my sixth form years.

"Thirty-nine, and in exile," he said with a bitterness to his voice that was hard to miss.

"Hitler…" I said, making the obvious assumption, given he was an Austrian academic and Jewish.

"Yes, Hitler, and the Nazis, aberrations on humanity…"

"That's putting it mildly," I ventured. "Still the second world war put pay to them." For a fleeting second I found myself wondering if, as he had died just before the war, he was aware that the Nazis were defeated in the end.

"Yet, man learns nothing from his own history," Sigmund stated, which given the turn of geopolitics of late was hard to dispute.

"Not that I've noticed," I agreed. "Though that was before my time… So were you come to that, which makes all this make little sense," I added. Though the full realisation of just how strange all this was, was only just beginning to sink in.

"Troubling, is it not?" Sigmund noted.

"You mean that I find myself sitting in a rowing boat, noticeably short of oars, in the middle of the ocean, with no recollection of how I came to be here. Sharing that boat with the father of modern psychology, who beside being dead before I was born, also seems to know an usual amount about Japanese assassins. Oh, and I'm dressed like Captain Jack Sparrow, and nursing a hangover of epic proportions while I try to make sense of it all?" I sighed, and recovered a half empty bottle of rum from the bottom of the boat, concluding that if I was dressed like a pirate I may as well drink like one.

"Indeed," said Sigmund Freud, the aforementioned father of modern psychotherapy.

"Well, I assume I'm dreaming." It seemed the logical conclusion by this point. I then pulled the cork and took a draft of rum which tasted like the bilge water it had been laying in. I wiped the mouth of the bottle on my sleeve and offered it to the Austrian head-shrinker.

"That would seem a reasonable assumption, except for two things," he said by way of reply, after politely shaking his head at the proffered bottle.

"What two things?" I asked.

"Well, for one, if you are dreaming then I am no more than a figment of your subconscious, which would imply you have a deep inner yearning to understand some intrinsic truth about yourself."

I took another swig of rum, which tasted little better than the first. "Sure, sure, that makes sense I suppose, and the other?" I nudged.

"Well, in my experience, dreams are an expression not of the ego, or the super ego but of the id, and can usually be attributed to deep-seated insecurities and unresolved sexual feelings towards your mother. In which case, we should ask ourselves, why are you dressed as a pirate?" he posited.

"What's my mother got to do with anything?" I asked, though he was right about the pirate thing. It was bothering me as well. I mean, I liked the aesthetic, who doesn't? Pirates are fun, cool and let's be honest here, sexy. There is something innately attractive about the aesthetic. Big coats, corsets, flintlocks, cutlasses, tricorns, frilly shirts and that certain windswept but interesting look. Pirates, if you discount the whole vicious murdering bastards with rickets thing, are awesome. But putting swashbuckling antiheros to one side, if I was sure of anything it was that I did not have unresolved sexual feelings towards my mother.

"It is always the mother when the subject is male," Sigmund stated in a point of fact way.

"Are you trying to imply I am dressed like a pirate because I have sexual feelings about my mother? Because I'm not and it's not. I'm damn sure I don't have an Oedipus complex." I said it a little louder than I intended.

"But of course you do. Every man has an Oedipus complex. As well as a deep rooted desire to return to the womb, but regardless, tell me, is it the case that you were you breastfed as a child?" he asked me, in a perfectly straight tone of voice, like it was the kind of question you could ask anyone.

"I'm not answering that…" I said firmly.

"Why not, do you not think it is relevant? Because I assure you it is," he said evenly.

I took another swig of rum before answering, which did nothing to ease my annoyance. "You may have been obsessed with your mother, Sigmund, but not everyone is."

"Nonsense, of course you are, otherwise why would I, of all people, be here in this row boat with you, dressed as you are, as some fanciful notion of a pirate, in the middle of this endless ocean?" he asked me in all seriousness.

"………." I said, or rather, didn't.

"Your choice not to comment alone is verification

of my posited explanation. Perhaps that rum bottle you clutch at is just another substitute for a nipple on which to suckle?"

"...................." I said, wide-eyed at the suggestion, then despite the absurdity of his suggestion I took another drink.

"Of course, there is a further explanation. Which is to say that you are not in fact dreaming, that you are dead and that this is in some way your purgatory. So here you are, cast adrift on an ocean of despair, a pirate with no ship, a fast depleting supply of rum and a deceased psychotherapist asking you questions about your latent sexual feelings towards your mother. Perhaps you are even now on the point of death, and this is the last firings of neutrons across your unconscious mind as you slip from life. In which case we come back to the first question, why are you dressed as a pirate?"

"..............................." I didn't say. I drained the last of the rum and in a fit of irritation threw the empty bottle over the side.

"Come now, we will get nowhere if you refuse to speak," Sigmund Freud said to me.

I stared back at him a little wide-eyed, and somewhere at the back of my mind something else seemed wrong, but I could not place it for a second. "Tell me, do you normally braid your beard?" he added as it struck me I had thrown away the empty rum bottle. The bottle that now that lay half full at the bottom of the boat. The self-same bottle I had thrown away. Yet, now I thought about it, there had been no splash and now the half full bottle lay at the bottom of the boat once more, lolling about in the bilge water.

I grabbed the bottle, popped the cork and took another draft of briny rum.

"This is a dream," I said, sure, thanks to that bottle that this was the truth of it.

"Probably," said the cat that was curled up next to Sigmund. It yawned playfully, then added, "But is it yours, or his?"

"Mine," I said firmly, perfectly happy to accept that the cat had spoken, because this was a dream after all. "And now," I added, somewhat drunkenly thanks to the rum. Then I quite deliberately paused to drain the bottle once more and throw it out to sea. Where, pointedly, it failed to make a splash again. Then I pointed at the psychotherapist in an accusative way and continued, "And now, I'm going to wake up."

Then, I quite deliberately threw myself out of the boat.

There was a definite splash as I tumbled off the pedalo and into the boating lake. Luckily it was only a few feet deep so as I was sharply woken from my drunken stupor. I managed to make it to my feet and stand waist deep in the somewhat slimy water. People were laughing from the side of lake where the man hiring out the pedalos stood next to a small hut with a raggedy skull and crossbones flying from it. Somewhat embarrassed at having fallen asleep on a pedalo, not to mention then falling out of it, I waded through the water to catch the craft which my fall had sent drifting away from me…

Embarrassed, and soaked to the skin, I determined no matter how fine an idea it may have seemed at the time that I would never get drunk and mess about on a pedalo after watching Pirates of the Caribbean again.

Though I couldn't shake the weirdness of the dream from my mind. Why the hell had I dreamt of Sigmund bloody Freud? And why did I now have an overwhelming urge to ring my mother?

Sigmund regarded the cat. "Why do you always do that?"

"What?" the cat purred innocently.

"Is it yours or his?" Sigmund scolded. "Clearly it is theirs, as they always wake up in the end!"

"Really, but if they always wake up, yet you are still here... then is it them waking up or are you still dreaming?" the cat said archly, then got up, stretched, and sauntered off to the far end of the boat where a small oddly glowing doorway, or perhaps it was just a cat flap, appeared and the sound of a piano being played came through it. With a momentary glace back at the psychotherapist over its shoulder, and a curling of its tail, the cat wandered through into the lively bar room beyond.

Sigmund sat in his boat for a while and let his gaze traverse along the horizon. He tried not to think about where the cat had gone, or why he was in the boat. He had been in the boat a long time and in that time he had reconciled himself to the thought that this was his own form of purgatory. Cast adrift on an eternal sea, analysing dreamers when they appeared before him for their short sessions.

He knew why of course, he had after all always wanted to be a pirate when he was a child, and his mother had never let him dress up as one.

It always came back to mothers, even for him.

There was a pop and a new dreamer appeared before him. A dreamer dressed in black silk that may have been pyjamas a moment before but as the dreamer started to observe his surroundings morphed into other garments, though similar in some regards to night wear…

"Arh, you're a Shinobi," Sigmund said.

"I think I'm a ninja actually," said the dreamer, though they were clearly confused.

Sigmund peered at the man over his spectacles. "Yes, that is what I said, but regardless, tell me now, do you remember being breastfed as a child?"

THE TOWER

You never notice the tower at Southbridge when you first see the town.

You never noticed the tower at all, most of the time. It has a way about it. A way that allows it to slip out of sight behind nothing in particular, even when you're looking straight at it. For reasons that are hard to explain, when you're looking at it your eyes would inevitably be drawn to something else. Mundane things would strike you as far more interesting than the tower ever could be. Not that it would be something you'd think about. You never really thought about the tower at all which was, I suspect, the point.

Travellers, that rarest of commodities passing through town, would often find themselves bemused should the tower be mentioned in passing by a local. Much as the locals would be equally bemused if a traveller asked about the tower. Generally, they would assume such inquiries were about the inn in market square. This was, it must be said, not an unfair assumption. The Inn was after all called 'The Tower' and had a neatly crafted, painted sign for the benefit of those who couldn't read, hanging on hinges that squealed as it blew back and forth in even the lightest of breezes. This occasionally wrong assumption was seldom pointed out by anyone. After all, someone mentioning 'the tower in the market square', was likely as not referencing the inn, not the two-hundred-foot-high, slender, wand-like tower that dwarfed every other building in the town and had an evening shadow which should've fallen across the whole square.

Well, at least, it would've done if the tower actually cast a shadow, but as the local explanation goes 'it chooses not to'.

The locals of course knew the tower was there. It'd be impossible to live in the non-shadow of a building so spectacular and be unaware of its existence, no matter how unobtrusive the tower chose to be. But the thing is, when you see something every day, which does everything it can to encourage you to ignore it, you learn to ignore it.

Besides, "It's just there. It ain't like it makes a habit of moving about or anything," Rudolf the baker's lad told me once while we were taking an eighth day's afternoon laze by the fountain across the square from the tower. A ritual young men of the town engaged in every eighth day in the hope that one of the young women of the town might join them. Which is something I can tell you from sad experience seldom happened, as the young women tended to gather by the other fountain across the square in the hopes, the wisdom of years has taught me, that one of the young men of the town might join them. Such has been the dance of courtship in Southbridge for generations, neither side willing to meet the other halfway. Though in fairness halfway between those fountains is the tower.

Now it must be said that Rudolf the baker's lad wasn't a deep thinker. In the scheme of things he was a lad perfectly endowed in the brains department for rising early, kneading the dough, thinking about the lass who worked in the taproom of The Tower Inn, and trying to guess the likelihood of her coming by the fountain that afternoon. If, however, you wanted to discuss comparative philosophy, he wasn't really the lad for you. So, his observations on the tower were little more than regurgitated local wisdom. The kind of wisdom common to most of the good burghers of the town. Much the same as if he'd looked up at a red sky one evening and told me, "There will be rain on the morrow." But that said he was right enough. The tower, well, it was just there…

You see, the tower had been a fixture in Southbridge and had been for longer than anyone could remember, and if pushed they'd probably tell you it had been there longer than their long dead grandfathers could remember. It was 'just there', and had been 'just there' for a long, long time. This in no way explained a damn thing about it to my mind, but then in fairness I wasn't a local, and as the collective wisdom of the townsfolk would have it, you have to humour people who seemed a little over impressed by a two hundred foot tower of gleaming white stone, that somehow managed to be unobtrusive in spite of itself. They explained such interest in 'the tower' by that other piece of oft spouted Southbridgian wisdom "Outlanders, they be a bit strange in the head…"

To give the locals their due, they'd seldom say such a thing in front of an outlander. It was, however, exactly what they would say behind your back and whether you were in hearing range or not. Just so long as they weren't looking you in the face at the time.

It may seem strange to you that I was considered an outlander, born and raised, as I was, within half a day's walk of the town. But Southbridgian's are an insular lot, and to their mind to qualify as a local you had to be born within the non-shadow of the tower. This was an unspoken but never the less important rule in the collective consciousness of the townsfolk. While if pressed they wouldn't admit it, a man could move into town within a few days of his birth. He could be raised there, educated there, work an honest job, meet his soulmate, marry, father children, grow old, die and indeed be buried on cemetery hill. But the good folk of Southbridge would still chisel into his tombstone, 'Here lies John Dodd, a nice bloke for an outlander, but he'd some funny ideas'.

So outlander I was, though I'd been coming to Southbridge since I was nothing but 'a blooming hindrance' according to my Dar. I'd ride into town perched on the back of Dar's wagon when I was sent along with him because Mar didn't want me under her feet all day. Of course in those days coming to town was a great adventure for the youngster I was and I would tell him earnestly, "I'll be helpful, Dar. I'll help you unload, and, and, I'll not get in the way or anything, honest I won't…" And my Dar would grumble and complain for the look of the thing, but tip me a wink, smile and tell me later he liked company on the long wagon ride.

Along the way Dar would tell me long stories that seemed to have little point but made me laugh anyway. It wasn't that his stories were funny, it was more the way he floundered about in the telling of them, the way he kept losing his thread. He wasn't a great teller of tales my Dar, but he told them with all the gusto and enthusiasm that only a father can have for a tale told to his son.

On those long trips the wagon would plod along the occasionally passable road of hard packed earth, with the very occasional stretch of cobbles laid for a few yards. Once, the road was paved and cobbles merely formed the under layer. But that was hundreds of years past in the days of the old empire. Like so many things left over from the old empire, the road was on its last legs, the paving stones long since 'borrowed' for one building project or other by enterprising vandals. Yet even without the top stones, old empire roads remained better than others if you wanted to get from one place to another. Not that anyone went much of anywhere. The old empire had built things to last, even if lasting meant clinging on by its fingernails to the edge of a roof.

The road ran along the bottom edge of the forest that grew wild and ragged beyond the farms of my family and our neighbours. In the other direction it went to Provincia, the old provincial capital back when the empire was still a thing. According to Dar, it was now a collection of aging ruins with a small village nailed round it, or perhaps he said 'to it'. Though I'm sure he'd never been there himself. It was a good thirty miles away after all. Aside the odd tinker and the occasional travelling troop of entertainers who showed up from time to time, no one much came down that road these days. In theory Southbridge and farms like ours around it were all part of some duchy or other, but as whomever the duke may be no one sent any tax collectors our way, which no one seemed much inclined to mind. A few miles past the end of my father's land the road turned south proper away from the forest edge and cut through the gentle hills before it came down into the northern slope of the valley where Southbridge nestled along the banks of the river.

As you would expect, for a boy raised on a small country farm, my first sight of a town the size of Southbridge came as a shock. I'd have been five or six at the time, and had never been further than my mother's yell from the farm house, though in fairness my mother could yell a long way. Up till then, the most people I'd ever seen at one time was during harvest when my dad would bring in a few labourers, or when a troop of gypsies passed our land, which was more often than not the same time. Southbridge was a thriving metropolis in comparison, all the more so on market day. But it wasn't all the people, or the plethora of buildings built on top of each other that took my breath away. It was the sheer noise, the smell and the constant activity. From the hill side the town looked like an upturned ants' nest, stretching either side of the white stone bridge from which it got its name. The bridge was another relic of the old empire, but in better repair than the road because even the dimmest procurer of stone thinks twice about taking down the sides of a bridge. The whole place was too big, too busy, too full of life, noise and smells that would turn a cow's second stomach.

I loved it instantly. Show me a child who wouldn't.

I remember that first visit to Southbridge vividly. Sitting on my Dar's cart like a little prince riding a carriage into town. Looking down from on high at all the interesting and strange people milling around. Then watching Dar discuss the prices for his crop, the cost of his tac and other supplies, with the dozen or so stall holders around the market square, talking a language that seemed foreign to my ears as he haggled over the price of three yards of cloth and some needles for my Mar. Then he came back to the cart with a paper bag full of magic he called 'toffee' he had procured for me from a sweet stall. I remember trying to help him load a barrel of wheat beer at the end of an hour of trading with this stall or that and being roundly told to go sit back on the cart. I even remember sulking for a while, before I remembered the magic bag of 'toffee' and cheering up profoundly as I slipped some more of that magic into my mouth. The whole visit lasted no more than a couple of hours. Even with time for Dar to share a tankard of beer with another farmer or two outside the Inn. Then we were packed and heading back over the bridge and home. Those couple of hours seeming to stretch on forever, yet pass in moments. In the way such things do to a child.

As we headed up the hill and Southbridge slowly faded behind us, my Dar turned to me, playfully jabbed me in my ribs and asked me the question he'd doubtless been dying to ask.

"So, did you notice it?"

"Notice what?" I returned, puzzled by his question.

"The tower in the market square," he replied, winking at me.

"Was that the name of the inn?" I asked. A vague recollection of a sign with a picture faded by too many years in the sun came to mind.

Dar laughed, smiled at me, and continue to laugh for a minute or so as he guided the cart further up the hill. Eventually he drew it to a halt on the cusp, turning it slightly to the side of the road so we were looking back down the valley. Then he pointed down at the town and directed my vision to the middle, where the market lay.

"That tower!" he said pointing out what was suddenly the most obvious building in Southbridge. And for a moment, just a moment, I saw it plainly. The great rising circular tower that dominated the town that lay in the shadow it neglected to cast and raised up towards the havens…

I was young, so I never asked Dar how come he could always see it so plainly, when the tower hide from the perceptions of others. Thinking back now, I've come to suspect it was something to do with him looking with the eyes of a child, the ones he kept in a small leather bag around his neck. But some mysteries are never solved…

For those of you who have travelled a little further afield than a six year old farmer's son, a little perspective on where Southbridge is may help you to get a clearer picture of the town. Though I appreciate travelling a half day's cart ride from your home does count as both adventurous and worldliness in some quarters no matter your age. But to those who spread their fettle a little further afield, and who concern themselves with a world of kingdoms and empires, a bit more information may prove to be enlightening.

The town of Southbridge is on the southern bank of the river Taine in what in the days of the old empire was the Comorian province. One of the last great provinces of the old empire created before it fell into decline. To the north lay the ruins of the old provincial capital of Comoria. Which as you may of noticed earlier was not very imaginatively named. This may have been an early harbinger of the decline of the old empire. When you run out of murderous butchers, or as the old empire called them glorious heroic generals, to name cities after your civilisation is starting down the slippery slope of decline. I will admit this is not the most eloquent of theories, but I believe when you start struggling to find new murderous butchers to lead your armies, someone else will undoubtedly find their own gloriously heroic leaders, or as the empire would have called them murderous barbarian butchers, and start chipping away at the shining light of civilisation, or the tyrannous oppressors, depending on your point of view.

This is all ancient history of course, the old empire long ago declined to nothing more than a few cities with lots of history, vague feelings of superiority, and little else. Most people would be hard pressed to point out the empire on a map. Which is a shame since the best maps were of course still made in the empire. Possibly because when you used to own most of the world, you get very good at drawing pictures of it. At any rate it is over five hundred leagues from what remains of the empire to the old Comorian province, and most people living in Comoria would struggle to find the province on those same maps. Not for lack of intellectual prowess, I should mention, but simply because Comoria was now a collection of small kingdoms and large dukedoms.

A word of explanation may be in order about the difference between a large dukedom and a small kingdom. A small kingdom is made up of several very small dukedoms. Whereas a large dukedom is one where the Duke is powerful enough not to bother with all that tiresome paying homage to kings and rules the land himself. Some large dukedoms are larger than small kingdoms, and most dukes of large dukedoms spend much of their time contemplating how to get the rulers of small kingdoms to accept them as king of their own realm rather than just mere dukes, despite the clear disparity in power between a large dukedom and a small kingdom. Often this involves convincing a small kingdom by means of war, usurping, beheading of small kings and taking of their thrones. Which generally leads to the small dukes of the small kingdom scattering from those kingdoms and trying to do some usurping of their own. Meanwhile the kings of small kingdoms look down their noses at mere dukes of large dukedoms and try to become larger kingdoms by means of marriage, patronage and alliance forging. All of which is just another form of warfare, particularly the marriage part. Though it has to be said, most kings are just as happily use the more direct form of warfare, particularly if they don't like the look of the prospective bride.

Wars happen. Rulers change. Kingdoms rise and fall.

Meanwhile most border towns change hands every generation or so, after the seemingly obligatory rape and pillaging. Then settle down to pay taxes to the new lord of the realm. Wiser would-be kings try to restrict the rape and pillaging to a minimum in order to avoid too much upheaval and get on with the import matter of taxation, which is another form of pillaging but more organised, and the profits flow directly to the king's purse rather than getting distributed among the rabble.

Southbridge, as you might guess, is such a border town. It borders the young kingdom of Sitifia, which has existed for longer than anyone can remember. The Grand duchy of Nordland, which is not particularly grand in size but has a duke whose ego is considerable. And the kingdom of Frank. Frank is currently ruled by

King Frank the Third, whose grandfather liked his people to remember who is in charge, so took the unusual step of renaming the kingdom after himself. The third King Frank is, like his father before him, a traditionalist, at least when it comes to the matter of the naming of kings, so decided to name each of his children Frank with a view to keeping the dynasty going. This, so I've been told, is somewhat to the distress of Princess Frank, the current heir apparent.

Exactly which of these three realms currently has Southbridge under its banner is doubtless a matter of heated debate between those rulers. Debate that has occasionally threatened to move to a more direct form of diplomacy via sharp bits of metal. Southbridgians themselves, however, seldom if ever express any opinion on the matter and consider themselves to be independent of all three, while remaining perfectly happy with the status quo regarding the town's status. This in part is because the current state of affairs means none of the three kingdoms send tax collectors to Southbridge for fear of antagonising the others.

Now, all this may strike you as an odd state of affairs. If it doesn't, perhaps it should... But what perhaps should strike you as even odder, and I say this in plain view of my own hindsight, is that I, a mere farmer's son, happens to know all of this. Perhaps it would help if I tell you that Political History, Structures and Relative Comparisons of Feudal Economic Structures, is considered an obligatory class in the old schoolhouse in Southbridge. That along with English, Maths and Thermodynamics.

As I say, I say this in hindsight. It never struck me, or indeed any of my classmates as odd at the time. It was just the stuff they made us learn…

Before my school days, trips to Southbridge were a rare thing. My Dar may have liked the company but my Ma liked chores getting done more and Dar could only take one of us along each time. Being the youngest of four, three sons and a daughter, and Dar only going to town once a month or so, made such trips a rare thing. Besides which, if Dar needed a hand with lifting stuff he would take my oldest brother Dan, whom Dar wanted to 'learn the farm' which meant, among other things, knowing the knack of buying and selling at market. It also meant learning how best to chew sticks of straw and the correct way to lean on gateposts. Things my brother Dan excelled at.

Sometimes if he had Dan busy around the farm, which I always assumed meant there was a gatepost that needed propping up for a few hours, Dar would take Jeb for the heavy lifting. Jeb was good at lifting, as long as you told him what to lift and where to put it, in a steady slow voice. Jeb got his head banged as a baby, or so my Ma claimed. So Jeb was, as she put it, 'solid but slow' or as my Dar was more inclined to say 'thick and idle', but his heart was generally in the right place. Slightly left of centre, behind his rib cage.

My sister, Patty, only went to town if Ma was going, which was generally about once a year. Most of the time she helped Ma around the house, and with the chickens. Beasts which require an inaudible amount of work considering they generally just scratch around the yard and squawk at you if you come too close. Patty, it seemed to me, spent most of her time dreaming of a handsome prince coming along to save her from the drudgery of it all. At least that was until she got a little older and started to think more in terms of a solid farmer's son with land to come in to. Handsome princes being something of a premium thereabouts, while you couldn't move for slow witted farmers' sons, with fair looks, a few dozen cows, and a working knowledge of haystacks. By the time those farm boys started looking at her appraisingly, she had already appraised them all and knew their value down to the last sheep. She was nothing if not pragmatic, my dear sister.

All this conspired so that while I was young I got to ride into town once or twice a year at most when Dar needed company more than help. Thus due to its rarity, the sublime magic called toffee and wondrous wide-eyed staring at everything, didn't wane for several years. I did however slowly get used to the sights and sounds of the town. Though I never got used to the weird way in which the tower could slip from your mind even when you were staring right at it. It must have been four years after that first trip, as we rode back towards the farm after a long day's haggling, that I realised I'd never actually asked my Dar anything about the tower. For all the constant spill of questions when we rode to and from town. The tower, both singular in its inconspicuous presence and its imposing domination of the town, had never caused a single question to come from my ever-inquiring now nine year old mind. Not in four long years.

This struck me as rather odd. Which in fairness many things seemed to strike me. But all of a sudden a dozen questions sprang instantly to my lips and spilled over each other in a garbled nonsensical outpouring of verbiage as we looked back at town from the hill as we always did.

My Dar laughed. Then told me to slow down and start over with my 'incessant questionings'.

Several deep breaths later, as I tried to decide which of all my questions was the most important, I could feel them all slipping from my grasp. As if something was forcing me to forget them, even forget I was curious about the tower in the first place. With all the reserves of willpower a nine-year-old can muster I forced myself to remember at least one question, while holding my breath until I thought I'd turn blue, in order to get it out from between my lips.

Then carefully, slowly and pronouncing every word as exactly as I could, I asked him the most burning question I could hold on to. "Dar, who lives in the tower?"

My Dar smiled at me and turned to look back at tower again. Then, while holding the pouch around his neck, he smiled at me and joked, "I'm guessing you're not referring to Old Harry and his wife down at the Inn in market square?"

I gave him my best annoyed stare, while feeling somehow strained as if the question, even now it had been asked, was still trying to slip away from me. The pressure to just drop the question and forget it had even occurred to me was almost overpowering. I forced myself to breathe deeply once more and just nodded in reply.

Dar grinned, though I can remember seeing his hand clutching even tighter at the pouch round his neck as he spoke once more, and seemed to visibly wince. "Then if you mean the other tower. The tower. Well then, that would be the wizard who lives there, son. The demandable wizard of Southbridge."

I remember wanting to ask him more, but the day was getting on and we still had far to go. Besides which, questions kept slipping from my mind. Even remembering him telling me about the wizard seemed a hard fact to grasp hold of. I had to force myself to remember what he had told me. I even made up a little rhyme to keep the thought in my head.

The wizard lives in the tower
In the tower the wizard lives
The wizard lives in the tower
I know 'cause my Dar said…

I'd sing that to myself for hours on end sometimes. I didn't know why, though I have the strangest memory of Dar telling me the rhyme himself, and making me sing it to him on the road back to the farm that day. Dar was strange like that when it came to the tower, unlike anyone else he seemed to think it was important for me to know things about it. Yet I gave it little thought at the time, nor did I think about that strange pouch he wore around his neck. The one with the eyes of a child in it, as he always told us. Though I never looked to see if that was really the case or not, not for many years, not until I understood a lot more about the world and the tower, and by then I was looking for something else.

It was two years later, after harvest, because harvest always came first, that I was packed off to Mrs Broccoli's boarding house for children, in order to begin my schooling. In those two years I doubt the tower occurred to me all that often. Though I would find myself singing that little rhyme to myself at the strangest times. The stream of questions I'd had that day never reoccurred to me. Thinking back now I would guess on some level I chose to avoid thinking about the tower just to avoid that feeling of being forced not to. I suspect that in this I was far from alone. I further suspect that is part of the trick to it all. The tower doesn't like you thinking about it so makes itself hard to think about, and eventually you just get used to not doing so. Though I think Dar was always the exception to that rule. He only didn't think about the tower because he chose not to, not because it made him do so. Not that I understood why that was the case back then.

School was a strange new world. School and town life in general. I wasn't the only country boy to find himself packed off with two changes of clothes and a bag full of pencils after harvest that year. Indeed, the influx of 'sheep prodders' as the town kids called us, was an annual event. So that first week I not only left home for the first time, to take up residence in a room full of beds and the stink of the unfamiliar, but I also joined my first gang. This too was part of a tradition in Southbridge. The prodders vs the bridges, a war that had been fought for generations with sly trips, digs in the back and scattered books.

It didn't help that us 'prodders' started our schooling two years after the townies. Nor that we did so in stints of six weeks at a time between harvest and sowing, while the townies attended school three days a week all year round. We started behind, and were always rushing to keep up. Though I found applied logic, the theorems of dead Greeks, and composite chemistry, easy in comparison to most of my fellows, I still found myself behind the curve of townie education for the first year or so. Yet in time I found myself at the head of the class more often than not, a position, in the strange society that is a classroom, which brings its own problems. Being the smartest kid in the class and a 'prodder' to boot made me unpopular with both the 'townies' and my fellow farm boys alike. But I was the youngest of four and had grown up avoiding the disapproval, fists and feet of my siblings. As such I was equipped to deal with the results of my unpopularity and even though I was small for my age I'd worked on the farm for long enough to develop the kind of stockiness that lends itself well to the odd brawl when necessary. After a couple of fights with bigger boys who were unwise enough to judge strength by height alone, a truce was soon declared, followed by de'taunt and finally acceptance.

It was in my second year, as the last few days of second harvest dwindled, that the headmaster of the school came to my father's farm and took my parents off to one side. Dar, as I remember, looked less than happy about this, yet at the same time he'd an odd look of resignation about him. I didn't know at the time but I'd been marked out by the headmaster as 'a lad to watch' whatever that meant. As such he had come to suggest to my parents I attend school full time and move into town to live at the school itself.

I remember the argument that ensued. My Dar, whom I had seldom heard raise his voice before, was adamant that this was not going to happen. Mar was proud and kept saying 'maybe it for the best'. But Dar just argued back that 'no kid of his was going to end up in that damn tower!' Which made no sense as that wasn't what was being suggested but aside the raised voices I could hear nothing more that was said in that room. In the end the schoolmaster left looking disgruntled and no more was said about the prospect of me going to school full time.

Seasons turned, as they are wont to do, and not much happened.

Not much ever happened in Southbridge. Indeed, if the history I was taught at school was anything to go by, nothing ever happened in Southbridge. While we learned about the rise and fall of civilisations, war and political upheavals, these were all events of the distant past, in distant places. Southbridge existed in its own little bubble it seemed to me. A distant outpost of the old empire that even the old empire failed to recall. The town and the surrounding hamlets and farms, just plodded along in its isolated remote way.

'Forgotten about, or perhaps just slipping from the mind of the world beyond the forest and the distant hills that surrounded the region, almost like the tower in the centre of the town slipped from the mind of those who lived there.'

I wrote that in an essay for humanities, three years or so after that first visit to the farm by my headmaster. At the time it seemed an obvious insight. Yet it caused such a ruckus when I handed in that paper.

'Old Kemp' was a retired miller who spent most summer afternoons nursing a pint outside the Tower Inn on the philosophical benches with the other retired men of the town. In winter they would retreat to the warmth of the tap room and do much the same. But twice a week he taught humanities in the schoolhouse and droned on to a bored classroom in much the same way as he droned on to his friends at the pub, though with less actual interest in his subject matter.

Many of our teachers were like 'Old Kemp', retired tradesmen and women who did a few hours at the schoolhouse imparting knowledge to the next generation of Southbridgians. Schooling is, it strikes me, the art of distilling old knowledge to young minds. The schoolhouse in Southbridge did this in the most literal way. Most of our textbooks were older than our teachers, or our teachers' teachers come to that. 'Old Kemp' was in some ways the worst of them, as he could make any subject seem dry and dusty with age. Indeed, I only ever saw him excited by anything once and that was when I put in that essay.

I was held back after class, and made to wait while the headmaster was summoned. An occurrence that did not sit well with me. I was due to meet Rudolf and the others at the fountain and we were certain, despite all previous evidence, that a couple of girls from the other fountain were going to come over and talk to us this time. In fairness we were certain this stupendous event would occur most every day, yet it always failed to materialise, but as I sat in the empty class room, regretting ever writing that damn essay, I was entirely certain that this would be that sainted afternoon the girls would finally wander over. The one afternoon in the last three weeks I wasn't going to be by the fountain with the other lads.

In short, I was cursing my foul luck.

The headmaster read my paper, then he read it again, fixed me with the kind of stare that make any school kid feel an urge to vomit when you're getting it from the headmaster. Then he nodded to 'Old Kemp' who nodded sagely in return, stood up and left the classroom.

All the while I just sat there waiting, a feeling of doom seeping over me, not least because I was certain one of the girls must have wandered over to the boys' fountain by now. They may even be talking...

The headmaster read the essay yet again. Then looked me square in the eyes and his face took on a look of resignation. As if there was some task he had to undertake that didn't sit well with him at all. I remember feeling worried by that look. No boy wants to see a look like that on the face of the man with a cane in his office.

Then he looked down at my essay, which by the way was titled 'Comparative philosophical outlooks on the possibility of things not being what they seem', a title I'd been proud of, but if you have a wit of sense about you will strike you as a strange title for an essay by a teenage boy from a small farming community, in some backwater which doesn't even know what country it's a part of.

In fairness, that's because it is.

The headmaster folded my essay in thirds and then, of all things, tied it with some string before taking the time to melt some sealing wax and stamp it with his signet ring. Which was undoubtedly an odd thing to do. Then he stood, gave me that same resigned look again and told me to follow him, mildly cursing under his breath, "I suppose I'll be the one who has to tell his Dar…" which I suspect I wasn't supposed to hear.

He led me out of the schoolhouse, across the square, and right past the boys' fountain, which I was pleased to discover, if only on this occasion, was noticeably sans girls as ever. But that moment of passing joy, which was based on nothing more than my selfish desires, was replaced with a strange sense of trepidation as the headmaster continued on to the very centre of the market square.

The centre that everyone walked around, and generally ignored.

That odd pressure that was always there when you looked at the tower seemed to build up at the back of my mind again as I sought to question where I was being led. Which is to say I knew where I was being led. I knew exactly where I was being led. I just didn't want to think about where I was being led, because it didn't want me to think about it.

I remember looking behind me for a moment and seeing my friends by the fountain. Not one of them was looking at me, very definitely not looking at me, as they too could see where I was going.

I snapped my gaze back around and felt a stab of pain just behind my forehead, and my vision blurred bright white for a second. Then I realised I was now standing next to the headmaster in front of a door. I'd never noticed that door before. But then why would I have done, it was a door in the tower and I never noticed the tower as such. So how could I notice the door?

The headmaster looked down his nose at me a moment. And I realised something else, the pained expression on his face was the mirror of my own. He'd had to force himself to lead me to that door, force himself to think straight enough to do so.

It was a perfectly normal looking door, I should perhaps add.

Is that a disappointment to you? That the door just looked much like any other you could find on any other building in the town. It was not much different from the door on my Mar n' Dar's farmhouse if I'm honest about it. I think it disappointed me at the time, as I tried to focus upon it. I think I suspected it should look like some grim doom laden portal. It should have had gargoyles around it and a huge bronze knocker clutched in a dragon's head. It should have been imposing. It felt imposing, but only because it didn't want me looking at it. Aside that one peculiarity it was just a wooden slat door, painted white, with a small brass knocker on it. No different from any other door you could find anywhere. But I guess you don't need to be imposing if no one can bear to focus their gaze upon you for any length of time without the overwhelming urge to not do so.

The headmaster handed me my essay, still tied and sealed. Told me to wait where I stood, and then he reached out, knocked smartly upon the door, turned and walked away.

I stood there clutching my essay, staring at the door that didn't want me to notice it and not daring to look away in case I forgot it was there. I felt a strange sense of determination wash over me suddenly. All those questions I'd wanted to ask my Dar came flooding back. All the questions I'd not been able to hold on to. What was the tower really? Who was the wizard? Why did people forget about the tower? What was it all really about? Why did the tower make us forget it existed? Those questions and a hundred more.

Time passed…

It may have been mere moments, it may have been days. I couldn't tell you.

Then slowly, the door opened, and a hand waved

me inside. What else could I do at that point but follow…

And then, everything I thought I knew, turned out
to be a lie.

Precipice

Through the mist, I see him. Glimpse him at least. A figure of shadow and darkness. Ethereal, unreal... Yet more real than anything in this strange begotten place.

It has been three days since the mist came.

Or perhaps three eons.

Time is... feels... fracture. That's not the right word, but it is the closest I can get.

Time is wrong, moments run in to hours, days pass without nights, or sunrise and the perpetual mist hangs in the air. Distance is impossible to judge properly thing seem to shimmer in the distance then be closer, or move further away, with no rhyme or reason. Sounds echo in dead air, indistinct and odd, and all the while there is are strange whimpering's and whisperings from voices detached of their owners.

'He is coming, he is coming.' the voices seem to say.

The voices out there in the mist, the fog, the heavy layer smog that muffles everything, every sound, every source of light. The voices of people and those of the not people.

The figure of shadow and darkness turns to me. A face without a face, without eyes, or with a hundred, locks its gaze upon mine. For a moment it is the face of my father, then my uncle, my brother, my mother. Then no one, then everyone. A thousand faces and none.

The figures beckons to me. Entreats me without words, without passion, to follow them through the mists.

So follow I do...

My footsteps on the wet ground follow no rhythm. I stagger as much as walk. I feel the tiredness of my limbs and an emptiness within me. A strange hollowness at my core. 'Am I dying?' I find myself wondering, 'Is this Death I follow? Is he leading me through this fog to my doom?'

And then I wonder... 'Am I already dead?' realizing as I do that this would explain so much.

Everything stopped when the stars changed. Everything I knew, everything we knew, thought we knew. Everything ended. Everything we took for granted. The power went out, taking with it, light, heat, and the safety-nets of civilization. Whatever was behind those plastic sockets on the wall ceased and everything beyond them too. Cars would not start. Phones went blank and stayed that way. Every technology we had long since ceased to truly understand failed at once and with it everything else. And the mist rolled in.

Or I died...

It would be simpler if that was true. That this is some strange netherworld beyond life. Maybe the voices in the mist and their unseen owners are the echoes of the real world. A world from which I have passed.

If I am dead, it all makes sense.

If I am dead I am a ghost wandering mist shrouded echo of the world that once was...

It would explain how everything just stopped. How the world seemed to end in one moment of change. I fell asleep in the old world and woke in the new. This mist shrouded purgatory I now inhabit, following the figure of death through a half-forgotten twisted landscape populated by the dark towers of industry that once belched out a chemical smog somehow more inviting that the wretched mists through which I now stumble.

I'm not dead though, I can't be dead. I would not feel this gnawing hunger in the pit of my stomach if I was dead. The damp cold air would not leach the heat from my body. My joints would not ache, my head would not pound. I would not feel the dozen little insidious cuts and grazes that criss cross my skin or the sting of the nettles that have grown everywhere in the mist.

No... I am not dead. Just the world I knew.

The figure leads on. I never gain on him, yet neither do I don't fall further behind. He is ever just there, that little way ahead of me, on the edge of my fog veiled vison. Wearing the mist like a cloak. Ever shrouded, ever indistinct, and ever beckoning me onward.

It leads me beneath a bridge, then past the broken remains of a traffic junction where lays an abandoned car, a burnt-out rusting wreck through which the wind whistles between its decaying remains. To my left on a patch of wasteland the corpse of a horse lays on the ground, its head still chained to a spike than hobbled it when alive. Flys buzz around it corpse, bloated things grown fat on decay. I stare fascinated by the grotesqueness of it. Then snap my gaze away as the horses' head turns towards me.

A trick of the light, this strange sickly light, no more, I tell myself...

The thing I follow moves through the junction then right. The road that way runs in parallel to the embankment upon which the trains once ran on now abandoned tracks. In turn, the embankment follows the river Tees as it murky waters sluggishly move towards the sea. Or did.

The river was always murky, a river with an industrial past, still tidal this far in land. From here I can hear the waters now, though I cannot see them.

I shouldn't be able to, I instinctually know this is true.

I know this road, this path. I know where it leads. Down through the Clarence's. Houses to the right, the embankment to the left. I know this road and you could never hear the river from it. Yet now I can. Is it the mist that carry's the sound to me? Or is the river wilder now. A torrent where once it was sluggish and placid. Had the river changed as much as everything else? Was it the source of the feted smell of decay on the wind? Or was it just one of many?

I follow on, down through the village of broken houses. It has been only days since the mist came and yet so many walls seemed broken, so many fences falling apart, a house with its roof burned out, shattered glass in broken frames. There is a feeling of degradation here, of decay, a feeling that seemed to stretch back to before the world changed. Before the world ended in so many ways. But now whatever balance was once here is lost. The worst is all that remains.

I follow the figure in the mist and as I do I remember this place, this road, and I remember where it leads. A sense of dread seeps over me and for a moment I find myself faltering in my pursuit.

They stop and turn to me once again. That face without a face and all the faces I have ever known, stares back and me and beckons me to follow once more.

So, follow I do.

Down past the row of shops set back form the road,

half untenanted even in the times before, now all empty shells blackened by fire. A group of youth haunt the place. Callow and shriven they stand by the husks of the off license taking no notice of me as I pass. Least I hope they don't. Perhaps they fall in behind me, matching my steps through the mist, their harsh whispers adding to my unease.

'He is coming, He is coming' they seem to say.

Do they mean me, I wonder. But no. I known they don't mean me, nor even the one I follow. He is no more than a harbinger.

The harbinger...

He leads me past the school where once young children once laughed, fought, played and ran in worlds of their imagination. The schoolyard is empty of such joys now. The things haunt it are the pale things that may once of been but are now no longer. Fragments of the time before that linger on in hopelessness and lack of expectation.

I shiver and turn my gaze away. I have no wish to look too closely at the things beyond the fence.

Further on the house sit back and an expanse of grass lays between the road and the buildings. The green that once grew they now thick with dark brambles that twisted and rolled as they grew. In amongst the thorns hang things that have been caught within. They rot there, filling the air with the stench of decay, sickly and sweet. I keep to the road and ignore the way the brambles seem to move in the wind that isn't there.

Plants don't move like that.

Plants are not predatory.

Plants do not creek and groan that way or moving like they are in a bad stop motion animation.

He I follow still waits ahead of me. Always just on the cusp of the mist, aways looking back and beckoning me on. I follow, still cautious, still afraid, yet fascinated, like prey staring at a cobra's dance. I follow as the mist seems to thicken and the road leads down into hollow before it breaks off to sweep right and under the embankment once more. The darkness of the tunnel dank and repulsive, but beyond it I see orange lights glowing in the mist.

The light is not welcoming, I want to stop, but my feel carry me onward. Compelled by some primal need to obey the summons. My breathing labored, a cold sweet on my back, I follow the faceless one of many faces under the railway. Water dripping from the ceiling, water and other things I don't want to think about. The stones groan under the weight of the world. Grinding against themselves, twisting in their mortar.

Beyond the underpass the great iron frame of the transporter bridge looms out of the fog. Torches have been hung from it, burn pitch and fat, giving off oily smoke that joins the murk. The great cradle swings in the dead air. Hanging at the midpoint between banks. A contraption of rope and sinew, wood and bone, bridges the gaps. Across this the figure walks, head to the cradle, there to awaits me.

I know this, I know not why I know this.

I know too, to follow him will mean my end, yet the urge to follow remains, the pull he exerts over me remains. As I move forward, fear gripping me. I hear voices in the windless air. Words more chanted than spoken but none of any language of which I am aware.

I turn now and see them. Emancipated figures dressed in rough spun yellow robes, skin so pale as to be translucent, greasy haired wretches, lost in some strange euphoric passion for an intelligence older than time. They move towards me, herding me onward, cattle like, towards the rope bridge. While he who I have followed thus far stands on the cradle. Watching me, waiting. Its face now that of dark-skinned pharaoh, with serpentine eyes. As I grow closer I see a flicker of a forked tongue flashing between bloodless lips.

He who came out of Egypt awaits me, as I step onto the span of rope and sinew. The wood, ancient and damp, creaks below me, and I look down at the turgid river, boiling below me. Running high, higher than I ever saw it in the times before.

The time before the stars changed. Before the world move on. Before the old ones returned.

Three days, has it only been three days, or has it been eons. Time has no meaning. Fractured and strange as it has become. The rules, the laws that govern reality, have become torn and ragged. Three days, three days since the mist came. Since the world slipped on it axis and those that had slept so long returned...

Is it everywhere, with the whole world shrouded in this thick cloying smog? If I turned and ran, could I run beyond it. Run back to a world of sanity and reason? I wonder...

But even as I wonder this I realise It doesn't matter. I realise it is too late for me now. I am at the bridge, I have always been coming to the bridge. I knew that. I had know that since the first morning when the sun didn't rise. I don't know how, I don't know why, but know it I did.

Perhaps the figure who has led me here is a delusion. Perhaps it is all delusion. Perhaps the world has not ended, perhaps things do not move in the water below me. Boiling, writhing, reaching out with grasping limbs like sinuous snakes. Tentacles that whip out and lash at the rope bridge as I cross it.

Perhaps I am mad.

But perhaps if I am, this madness is a gift. Is sanity ever something to cherish in a world on the precipice of oblivion?

The stars have changed. The old gods have returned.

Nyarlathotep awaits me on the cradle of the transporter bridge above a boiling Tees.

My end is here.

THE BALLARD OF JONNY
TWO BONES

The figure stumbled out of the saloon.

To say he stumbled is understatement, which is to say closer to a lie than a truth. He stumbled, he fell, he crashed out through the hinged half doors. He found his footing on the loose boards only to lose it again in his haste. Then he scrambles out into the night like all the demons of Hells are on his tail, which, from his prospective, ain't far from the truth…

So yes, let say he stumbled out of the saloon… Let's put it that way. He stumbled out of the saloon and kept right on stumbling, out into the dust and baked mud of a street that hadn't seen rain in an age. A street as dry as a devil's sense of humour.

Had there been just one damned soul out there to see him… Well… A blind one could have read the fear etched in his face. This was a man who had seen terrible things, some of them recently. Seen them and known all he could do was run. Yet in his fear he laid there, sprawled in the dirt. The one damned soul would've watched him laying there gasping. Gasping for air in the high desert where its baked so hot the air burns your lungs to breath it in the day and leaches all the heat from your body in the night. He lay there gasping, eyes, wide and wild, set on the very saloon doors he'd just burst through.

My guess, he lay there hoping he'd been struck by nothing more than some momentary madness. Some delusion brought on by being too long in the saddle. Too long alone in the high desert, just him and his horse, riding around out because… Well, I guess there's many reasons a man might be out in the high desert for a time. More reasons these days than ever, what with that damn fool war back east.

Brother killing brother.

Ain't no war less civilized than a civil one. Not that any war is. Makes you wonder don't it when those who call this nation theirs came here from their old world. An old world they left because they were sick of old grudges and petty kings. Left to come to this boundless land. The land of big sky's and near endless rolling prairie. A land with so much space and so much of that 'freedom' they prised so much… Yet in less than a generation they are fighting over who should have that damn freedom, over who controls the land. Fighting with so much anger, so much hate. Well, it all feeds back on itself don't it just. I reckon many a man has found himself before the darkest of gates thanks to that damn war, and many more will before they pay all that is due for the blood in the soil.

So sure, there are reasons why a man might ride out in the high desert for a time, but whatever this man's reasons were, they were his own. Can't say it matter all told. Not right then. Not with him spawled in the dust. As for whatever brough him out of the desert and into town, well I doubt that mattered much either. I doubt he was thinking much beyond the terror leaching at his manhood right then, even a damned soul could see that. But I dare say he knew right then coming into No Wells had been his last mistake.

No Wells… Did he not read the sign? He should have done, it's damn hard to miss. You'd have thought that would have warned him. The sign that used to read 'Two Wells' before they scrawled out the 'Two' and painted 'No' over it in something red that wasn't strictly paint.

Back when it was still Two Wells it had been a Prosperous little town. Out on the edge of the high desert, but not part of it. Not then. They were still digging silver out of the old mine workings up in the hills. There had still been good farmland about, good grazing for cattle… It was a layover on the road to elsewhere but a popular one. There were even rumours the railroad was going to cut through that way sometime soon. A prosperous town. A town growing, in the heartland of the mid-west.

Least ways it was. Then old Jonny Two Bones wandered in one day and warned the town folk the wind was about to change.

Damn old fool, thinking the white folks would thank him for his warning.

The Town folk didn't believe him. They remembered the other Jonny Two Bones, from before he walked out into the high desert. The Jonny Two Bones who would tell you anything for a finger or two of whisky. The Jonny who used to wave about his medicine staff, sing words he didn't believe in no more and tell you he was chasing away the bad spirits. The Jonny Two Bones who used to make them laugh, begging for a shot of fire. The Jonny Tow Bones they used to make dance by shooting at his feet.

Oh, how they laughed when they used to make Jonny Two Bones dance, before they drove him out into the high desert. It was a different Jonny Two Bones who returned. The 'crazy old Indian' had changed, not that they saw it.

The desperate drunk was gone, and Old Jonny had found the dignity he had relinquish for so long. He had remembered the eyes of Running Elk, he had remembered the pride in her smile. He was once more a serious man with purpose in his heart. He came and stood in the centre of Two Wells, banging his medicine staff on the dusty ground. Eyes painted black with soot and grease, feathers, and old bones in his hair, tied in with leather. He stood there yelling in the tongue of his fathers. He stood there calling out to his ancestor's. Calling out to the spirits beyond. Calling out to Cayote. Calling out to the firebird. Calling out to The Raven Woman. Calling out them and issuing a warning to the town's folk. The wind was changing. The Moon Maiden would soon turn from all and the waters of life would run dry.

A crowd gathered to watch the show. To point, and laugh, and curse him. Something in his manner accused them. Blamed them for what was to come. They knew, they felt it, and as is the way of the white man, they rejected it. As they rejected all the wisdom of the world they had replaced.

No one saw who shot Jonny Two Bones dead. No one saw the sainted stranger on the edge of the crowd, because no one cared to see. They were all watching Jonny Two Bones. So none knew who pulled the trigger, save the one who's hand lay on the gun, but who that was no one cared enough to ask. Not even Sheriff Danial's.

What was some crazy dead Indian to them anyway? "Old Bastard brought it on himself been drunk at noon in the middle of the street." Someone was heard to say. Others were quick to agreed. Not a one of them care to consider no one had seen him drinking that day. No one had seen him for almost a year. He had been out in the high desert, no one bothered to wonder why.

As I said, there's many a reason a man might spend time out in the high desert.

The old silver mine started to run dry not long after they put Jonny Two Bones in the ground. Not that they buried him. Not proper, not Christian. The Reverend said it would not be right to put him in the cemetery, what with him being a heathen and all. The town council paid a couple of miners to take the body out a way and dig a hole. Dare say they paid them enough to dig but not enough to make it deep. He was only a damn Redskin after all.

The first well dried up a few days later. The towns folk weren't too worried though, it happened from time to time and they set about digging a new one further out of town. There were mumblings in the saloon about 'That crazy old Indian' and the usual drunks saying he'd 'cursing us all,' but no one took such talk serious, not even the ones doing the talking.

They'd not finished digging a new well when the second one dried up a week later. About the same time the old preacher was found dead in his church. Slumped over his wooden cross, with strange marks on his naked back. Those that knew said they were lash marks. Sheriff Danial's said the old father must have been 'Some kind of flagellant' and that he'd 'Know their kind.' 'Shiver their own flesh in penance to the lord.' he told people and had the preacher taken down.

No one chose to ask where the old priest lash had gone when his heart gave out. Simple answers suit simple minds.

They found no water with the new well, or with the next and others started to die.

A miner came down from the old mines, saying he thought the seams were giving out, died in the night next to the girl he'd rented, with great gouged marks on his back that looked like someone's nails had raked trails of flesh from him. The girl claimed she had done no such thing. 'He didn't pay for no extra's' she told them.

They found the tanners boy drown in a barrel of piss, no one was sure quite how he'd fallen in. The tanner took it harder than a man should, and hung himself two days later, about the time people noticed what little water was left was running out. Also, about the time the first people started packing up wagons and heading further west. No one headed east, no one wanted to cross the high desert, and no one wanted to head towards the war that still raged beyond.

So it was the town started to die in slow cycles of desperation. Some folk tried to find the miners who buried old Jonny Two Bones. They got it in their heads that maybe the mad old Indian had put a curse on the town, and maybe if they buried him right, it might end the curse. As if the curses of one old Redskin could bring about such darkness in the world.

They never found out where the miners had dug his shallow grave. They had died in a cave in, a day before people first went looking. A cave in that closed what was left of the old silver mine.

The town continued to die and only those with no choice stayed behind hoping things would turn around. They waited and waited, and things got worse. Until the three rode in out of the high desert.

One of them looked like he knew where the bodies were buried, one of them looked like he was one of those bodies and the last, well she if she wasn't the sweetest thing that a man might ever see. Guess which one scared those who remained the most.

I saw the three ride in, and felt a fear the like of which I'd never known. I watched them from my perch in the bell tower. Watched them as the sky darkened and I felt the ill-wind that came with them.

They came from the east. From beyond the desert. From the killing fields of the war. From the slaughter and the hatred. That turmoil of raw emotion. They came from the place why lay the darkest aspects of humanity. They came from the root of it. Th root of man's inhumanity to man. That was what had birthed them. Or perhaps gave life to what they had become. What they were before, I know not.

They came on the dark winds that the Raven woman had warned Jonny Two Bone of. They came and left a trail behind them Cayote had both followed and foretold. They came in pain that made the firebird scream. They came, and the Moon Maiden turned her face from those who remained in Two Wells.

They came and in coming they feasted upon what remained of the town.

They came and it was they that changed the sign.

The Sheriff died first, at the stroke of Noon. Died with his lusting eyes locked on hers, thoughts of penetration in his mind, as she drove a knife up through his ribcage and into his heart. He would not be the last to die his eyes locked on hers. Nor would that look of twisted enrapture on his features be his alone. Ecstasy mixed with horror. Pain entangled with pleasure. Each life she takes ends in lingering agony on the blades edge. Slicing slithers of mortal's souls. Salting wounds with her own sweet desire.

There be no kindness in her.

The one who promised kindness was the first. He smiled as he slew, a smile that promised joy, forgiveness. If hers was a visage of lustful enticement his was one of sainted beauty. He offered the rapture, he offered righteousness, his was the hand of God bringing mercy to the world... Those he slew knew this. Knew it deep within themselves, even as his guns swung round to point their way. Even as his fingers pulled back on his triggers, they would greet their deaths as a blessing from God. It was only as the bullets struck. As pain erupted through them and their life blood sprayed forth. Only then did the thought ever occur to them, 'Which god...?'

If he was a saint, he was a saint of a darker god that the one who's church still bore the blood of its preacher upon its wooden cross.

I witnessed the realisation strike each of his victims in the last. I witness their moment of revelation. The horror that swept over them as they were dragged into eternity. The realisation that the saints 'good' was something both dark and primal. No less evil than the lust his female companion inspired in others.

Yet be it lust or rapture both were cleaner quicker deaths than that promised by the third of them. The one of the graves. The one who reeked with the sickly-sweet stench of bloated magots. His was a touch of corruption, of rot, of decay. He needed no blade nor bullet, just his touch alone could infect you with a festering of the flesh. Skin would blacken and blister. Putrefy on the bone. Eating away at the body as it spread through your veins. He was a plague made flesh.

All plagues made flesh. He was a lord of fly's and decay. To feel his touch was to experience the lingering, painful, death of the afflicted.

They came out of the east, an exaltation of ill deed and thought. Made by the horrors of war, they embodied the depths to which man can sink. Driven on the east wind they came across the high desert. They fell upon No Wells and the town died before them on its knees. All who remained there died as I witnessed the horrors the three brought with them from my perch in the bell tower.

It was two days later when the stranger rode into the dead town with only the damned to witness his arrival. Who he was, and why he came? Who knew or cared? It hardly mattered now as he lay in the dust, staring back at the salon doorway and watching as the three stepped out into the street.

She, the beautiful one, smiled at him, and for a moment I saw him weaken, he started to crawl towards her, but his desire to live must have been stronger than his lust, he stopped and climbed to his feet, stepping away, though his eyes were locked on hers.

As for me, I saw her for what she was, but what he saw was what she wished. I felt a pang of sympathy for him then. But he managed to break her gaze, only to find his eyes locked on her rapturous companion. But if the man saw any warrior of God before him, he knew that God for what it was and he turned to flee…

He got three steps before the saint's guns rang out, taking away his legs.

I watched as the three left the shelter of the awning and walked through the noonday sun towards their latest victim. She, walking like a flowing stream, every movement a seduction. The rapturous one with an elegant righteous stride. The third, like a contemptuous seeping from a blistered wound.

I heard their victim whimpering as he lay in the dust, Blood seeping from the ruin that had been his legs. He managed to turn himself over as they reached him. May the white man's god have mercy on him for that. Better to have died face down than staring up into their faces. The look of terror that crossed his face was more than the horror of the dying. I think he glimpsed the trio's true nature at that moment, as the third reached out a hand to smother him with sickness.

They stood around him in a triangle as if fascinated by what they had wrought. The man's body rotting in the sun, dissolving into a bubbling black goo of foul-smelling waste around already bleaching bones.

Time passed. Or didn't. What meaning has time to the damned.

Then the beautiful one turned and stared up at my bell tower, her eyes seeking mine. I tried to avert my gaze, but it is hard to turn one's gaze from beauty. Even beauty as terrible as hers.

She smiled at me, and in that fleeting instant her features changed from those of the tall blond, white woman before me, to those of Running Elk. Gentle, beautiful, Running Elk whose body I gave back to the sky so many years past. Running Elk who I had loved and who had loved me. Love and lain with me that one night under the blood moon, before the white men's soldiers came.

I remember my rage then. My anger. I remember seeking out the old ones, I remember the cave in the high desert. I remember Cayote telling me to turn back, and I did. I remember when I sought the cave a second time and the Raven Woman and the Firebird blocked my path. And I remember returning to the cave a third time. I remember Cayote's howl, the tears of The Raven Woman, the heat of the firebird, and the sadness on the face of the Moon maiden as I turned to seek her gaze before I entered the place of the ancestors. I remember faltering once again in my vision quest. I remember the moment I almost turned back. Then I remember seeing the face of Running Elk in the moon and the hardening of my heart once more.

I went down into the earth, deep into the darkness, to the place where the old gods lay. I remember offering them the hearts of my enemies in return for vengeance for my people. Vengeance for Running Elk. Vengeance for myself. And I remember the idol. Deep in the darkness, deep below the place of ancestors. The place the spirits of the ancestor's guard. Ancestors who's voices I had not heard, or had chosen not to hear, when they told me to turn back.

I remember how I opened a vein the darkness and gave my blood to the idol, to the thing of the idol. And then, then I remember nothing. For then I became something else for a while.

For years I walked amongst my enemy. I was their fool. I was the mad old redskin telling tales for fingers of whiskey. Whiskey to burn out the memory of what I had done. What I sought in the mountains. What I returned top seek once more, to seek to stop as the darkness grew in the east. Darkness feeding on the darkness at the heart of the white man. Jealousy and greed. War and lust. All the evil their war between brother had brought upon them, magnified and mixed with the blood I spilled below the mountain.

I came back and tried to warn them and paid the price.

And now they had come, and the beautiful one mocked me with the image of my lost love.

"Running Elk..." I heard the voice of the damned one in the tower say. My voice.

She who was not Running Elk smiled at me once more, but her face shifted back to the one she bore before. "Have you seen enough yet dead man?" she whispered seductively, louder than a cry.

The Sainted One, beside her smiled too, a halo of white light surrounding him. Though there was nothing clean about that halo. I could see the darkness behind the light. "Yes, dead man, come down from there." he said in a voice of pure temptation.

"Yessss, won't you join us now Jonny Two Bones?" the third asked. His word's containing the same sickly sheen as his skin.

I shrunk back behind the bell tower as they began to laugh, they knew I would not heed their words even as they spoke them. For they were ever cruel in their jests.

They summoned mounts that matched their visage and astride them rode off into the high desert. Leaving me there, the only ghost left to haunt the ghosted town of No Wells...

I watched them ride out into the high desert, I saw a fourth figure come out of the earth to join them. A figure called forth by all they had done so far. A figure that brought to my mind the words of a preacher of the white man's god. Words he once spoke to me from near the end of his great black book of his faith...

'And I looked, and behold a pale horse: and his name that sat on him was Death, and Hell followed with him...'

As he joined the three to become the fourth the figure turned back to look at the town and I saw his face.

His face was mine.

MANDRAKE

"Hendricks? He's dead, I believe. Murdered, if I recall correctly, a month ago. By members of his own coven, or so I am told."

This was a reasonable summing up of the facts. Which is to say, to the best of my knowledge that Jacob Hendricks, third Earl of Cleethorpes and mediocre occultist, was indeed deceased. As such, until any evidence to the contrary was presented, I laboured under the assumption that this was indeed the case. One does not as a rule presume notices of death in The Times obituary column to be falsehoods.

It is The Times, after all.

"Murdered…" Sir William Forshaw repeated, as is on occasion his habit. Forshaw is one of life's habitual repeaters, an affliction I find irritating in most people, but as one of his only vices when it comes to gentlemanly conversation, I remain inclined to forgive it of him because aside his capacity for repetition he is, in general, an insightful chap and a boon companion.

We all have our foibles, after all.

"Murdered…" he said again, his capacity for repetition failing to surprise me one iota. "Murdered… that's strange. I don't remember a trial."

"There wasn't one," I explained, taking a moment to fold up my copy of The Times. I placed it on the table beside me, steepled my fingers and added, archly, "There were… problems."

"Problems…" Forshaw repeated, then after a moment, his interest clearly piqued, "Problems… Oh, do tell."

As I warned you, a habitual repeater, irritating, is it not? But to continue…

"Well, for one thing, William, there was the problem with defining it as a murder," I explained blandly, feigning disinterest. In truth, I had been following the case quite carefully, but I am not one to play my cards with loose frivolity. My interest in the case was far from peripheral, but Forshaw was not to know that.

"Defining it as a murder?"

"Yes…" I said and reached into my overcoat for my pipe and tobacco. Busy work for my fingers. A man's fingers left idle can betray much, as I knew only too well. Besides this conversation promised to be expansive, as I had yet to determine Forshaw's own interest. His opening salvo of 'Mandrake, do you remember that chap Hendricks?' lacked any indication of why the subject had come to the fore. This I tried to determine as I held his eyes for a moment, but as this proved to be unilluminating, I took out my pocketknife and began scraping clean the bowl of my pipe and explained. "You see, there is a philosophical question at the heart of the matter, as well as one of law. To wit, is it an act of murder to kill a man, if you are commanded to do so by the man himself?"

"Commanded… by the man himself? You mean, Hendricks ordered someone to kill him?"

"So the members of his coven claimed and there was no evidence to the contrary. The question was posited by some therefore it was an act of suicide by proxy, rather than an act murder. The former is technically a crime, of course, but according to the statute, the greater part of the blame lays at the feet of the deceased, and while suicide is illegal, it is difficult to prosecute those who are successful in such endeavours. As for those who are unsuccessful, well, hanging the guilty party seems a tad redundant as a deterrent, wouldn't you say? Regardless, before Hendricks was 'assisted' to his mortal demise by his coven, he signed a letter of instruction to that effect."

"Signed a letter of instruction to that effect! Oh, come, Lucifer, you know as well as I do that signatures can be forged… I've done it myself at your behest a number of times in the past!" Forshaw exclaimed, which was decidedly indiscrete of him, given we were breakfasting at Charter House, a club frequented by, among others, our friend Sir Robert Peel, a man with an interest in legalities if ever there was one.

I should perhaps assure you that Forshaw's forging of signatures 'at my behest' were actions necessitated by circumstance and a minor illegality committed in order to expose a greater one. I shall decline to do so; one feels no need to coddle one's readers.

"Quite, Forshaw, quite. However, the signature in question was verified as Hendricks' own by Erskil."

"Erskil?"

"Scottish chap at the Royal Academy, done studies on handwriting. He claims he can spot any forgery. Sir Robert's runners have used him several times to determine the authenticity of documents…"

"Determine the authenticity of documents?" Forshaw blustered, looking momentarily flustered.

I let him simmer a moment or two as I packed my freshly scraped pipe with a decent shag, and struck up one of my namesakes to light it. I took a couple of strong draws to get the blaze going before I waved off his worries.

"Minor matters and I'm sure your own efforts in creative penmanship will pass any muster, my dear William. But regardless, in the case of Hendricks' papers, Erskil signed an affidavit stating it was Hendricks' own hand, something about the distinctive slope of the Hs, I'm told. But all this is by the by. The fact of the matter is be it by foul play, or his own hand by proxy, Hendricks is dead."

"Hendricks is dead…" Forshaw repeated, his habit starting to grind on me somewhat by this point.

"Yes, old chap," I said wearily. "One does, however, feel impelled to ask, why bring up the subject of a deceased magician of dubious portent?"

"A deceased magician of dubious portent. Well, you say 'deceased', but I bumped into him this morning in Marylebone while hailing a cab. To tell you the truth, he did look a tad green at the gills. It was why I mentioned him, you see. I know you and he had some contentions over the years. I thought you might be interested to know he was ill. I hadn't realised he was dead, which I suppose explains his pallid complexion."

"Indeed, it would," I said, somewhat disturbed by this revelation.

Jacob Hendricks 'had' been a third-rate dabbler, a professed spiritualist with no true understanding of the arts. He did, however, have a great deal of money, influence and power of the mundane kind. Thus, he had attracted fellow dabblers and want-to-be thrill seekers, as well as those cravens who always find ways to coddle up to men of influence. His 'coven' had about as much mystical power and insight as the average flower girl in Covent Garden. Slightly less than some who ply that market with their trade in fact. My 'contentions' with the 'Black Earl' as he described himself, had begun a year or two ago, when he tried to discredit my own rise, as I was, in his eyes, 'the wrong sort of magician'. Which is to say I lacked blood as blue as his own. Hendricks came from the school of thought that believed magicians should be the sires of noble heritage, and that any actual power they may possess was of secondary concern to their blood line.

In days past that was certainly true, at least, it could be held to be so. For books of arcane nature and access to such learning was well beyond the reach of those not born to money. It was a gentleman's pursuit first and foremost; actual power was of minor concern. There had not been a true sire of magic at court since the days of Dee.

In darker times, if one of the great unwashed exhibited any natural affinity for 'the arts', they faced persecution. The burning of witches and staking of warlocks was still commonplace as recently as a hundred years ago. Though I suspect those who lent their power to one of those reputable gentleman mages of the blood gained a level of protection. It was only with victory over Bonaparte, and the magical aid that won Waterloo in a day that public perception of practitioners of 'the arts' changed.

These are enlightened days. The age of industry, magic and enlightenment. Victoria's assent to the throne coincided with the rise of the second empire. What a man knew, what a man could do, these things meant more than ancestry.

At least that was the theory. Hendricks and his ilk clung to the old days. Hence the contention between he and I, and as such I had shed few tears at his passing.

He had even written to The Times on several occasions about 'mages of no breeding' and though he stopped short of brandishing my name in his missives, anyone who cared to read between the lines could see that his decrying of 'workman magicians', and 'upstarts with no pedigree' was a shot aimed squarely across my bows. Coming as these letters did just days after the Queen herself had granted me the right to proclaim myself to be Lucifer Mandrake, Magician by Royal Appointment. The fact this honour was earned by assisting with the 'wolf' problem at Balmoral the previous winter was by the by.

All of this was rather beside the point. However, it was clear to me that something rum and uncanny was in the works. Lord Hendricks for all his money, position and power, was no necromancer. I doubted he could reinvigorate the corpse of his daughter's pet hamster, let alone his own corpse, post-mortem. Either reports of his demise were grossly incorrect or there was a third hand at play, a hand with real power. It was clear to me this warranted investigation, for if someone was using magic for nefarious reasons it could undermine the profession.

More importantly, it could undermine my hard-won position. It would be a lie to claim I did not relish the notoriety and fame that came with a 'by Royal Appointment', nor the fees my services commanded.

"Where did you say you bumped into the oaf again? Marylebone?" I asked after several minutes of silence had passed between us. I had become somewhat lost in contemplations and the appreciation of a good rough shag.

Forshaw resumed reading his copy of the new periodical, Punch, though what he found so riveting in that publication escapes me. I doubted it would last out the year, focusing as it did on what passed their editorial staff as 'humour'. But as my pipe smouldered the last of the tobacco away, my thoughts had returned to the niggling issue of Hendricks.

"Marylebone," Forshaw dutifully repeated, then added, "on his way to Lords, I shouldn't wonder."

"The Lords, of course, what other use could a dabbler like Hendricks be but in the Lords!" I said with a lilt of triumph in my tone that was probably slightly unbecoming. It was clear to me however that a third hand was indeed at play, and now I suspected I knew why. The new Progressive Witchcraft bill going before the Lords next week. Someone, it seemed, was stacking the deck and a conservative like Hendricks made the perfect puppet, if you wished to stack the deck against the bill. Why else would anyone bring such a reactionary oaf back from the dead if not to scupper the decriminalisation of female magic.

I had to investigate, that much was clear. I had a vested interest in the statute of laws governing the practice of the arcane, after all.

"The Lords… no, not The Lords… Lords, the cricket ground," Forshaw said, interrupting my chain of thought.

"The cricket ground…" I said, doing my best Forshaw impression. "Oh, Lords of malevolent chaos save us. Forshaw, we're going to have to attend the match."

I cursed, with feeling.

Cricket is, as any right-thinking Englishman knows, the pursuit of louts, drunkards, ruffians and gamblers. And that, dear reader, is just the cricketers themselves.

The crowds that gather to watch the 'spectacle' are worse. The sport, if you can call it such, is a blight on society, rancid with corruption. Brawls between spectators are so commonplace some would have you believe events are attended by ardent fans just for the opportunity to drink and hurl insults at their rivals. Ministers, even Bishops of the Church have condemned it. The House of Commons once voted to ban the 'sport' altogether, only to have The Lords overturn the ban after six months for fear the louts would just move on to new pursuits. The prevailing argument at the time was that at least with them all contained in a cricket ground you knew where the louts were. Though as several sitting members of the Upper House are avid cricket 'fans' and attend matches regularity, one would not be misplaced in questioning their impartiality.

Yet, despite all this, somehow the sport of cricket itself remains terminally dull.

That said, if there was one place you are likely to find festering reanimated corpses engaged in a cruel mockery of life, other than the House of Lords itself, then it's probably a safe bet to look to the members' pavilion at Marylebone Cricket Club.

My course of action was therefore clear. I would have to face the tedium…

With Forshaw in tow, I left Charter House and hailed a Hansom to take us across London. A journey of some twenty minutes. Nineteen of these had passed when Forshaw made a puissant observation.

"It occurs to me that Hendricks knows you on sight old boy and had little love for you before he ceased to be actively among the living, as it were. It seems unlikely he will hold you in more regard since his passing," he said, as we rattled over the cobbled streets of west London.

"This is doubtless the case," I agreed, kicking myself that this thought hadn't occurred to me, but I was determined to discover the puppet master holding Hendricks' strings. To do so, inevitably, I'd need to get close to Hendricks. This omission was damn foolish on my part. Had it come to me earlier I could have taken a non-mystical means to disguise myself. There are advantages to such things. While a false moustache, a blond wig and sideburns may take both time and spirit glue to apply, they are, nevertheless, less arduous and time consuming than constructing a glamour from scratch. Creating a magical disguise of that nature quickly takes a great deal of skill. Projecting oneself into a new image is the easy bit, you must first create every aspect of that image in your own mind.

Every aspect.

Besides which, glamours have another disadvantage. Even if one takes the time and energy required to perfect such a disguise, magical disguises, no matter how carefully constructed, can be seen through by a magician of sufficient power if there is the slightest flaw. Hendricks never had the power to see through one of mine, but whomever his puppet master was undoubtedly did. Which presented me with both a problem and little time to consider a solution as we were mere moments away from arriving at Lords.

My mind raced through the many disguises I had

employed in the past but all of them were glamours best suited to other circumstances, at least among those glamours I knew well enough to slip into with minimal effort. Few of these were designed for polite society and, if hastily constructed, even one I knew well would be vulnerable to discovery. A truly complete glamour, one near flawless, was a glamour one had worn often and for extend periods. Long enough that you could inhabit that second skin seamlessly. It was this that made a glamour impenetrable, indeed eventually you can become the glamour in many respects, until even the most powerful could not see beyond it. Even someone powerful enough to raise the dead, for example… Only one of my myriad disguises fell into that category.

I had no choice it seemed. Lucifer Mandrake was too well-known a face and the antagonism Hendricks held for me was at odds to our mission. I needed to take on the aspect of one who none would suspect with prying eyes, third or otherwise. I was, however, reticent to do so for many reasons, but given the options I had, it seemed the only viable one and for all its drawbacks it did have one major advantage. In terms of the gentlemanly community of mages, it was a disguise that rendered me virtually invisible, after a fashion.

I closed my eyes, resigned to the decision my rash choice to pursue Hendricks directly had left me. Taking a deep breath to aid with focusing my mind on the task, I began and spoke quietly to Forshaw, keeping my eyes shut. I had no desire to see Forshaw go wide-eyed on this occasion. He'd witnessed the results of glamour magic many times, but had never seen an actual transformation to my knowledge. So I decided I should spare him an audience to his incredulity.

"Mr Forshaw, would you do me the honour of escorting my cousin Lucy Drake to tea at the MCC?" I asked, self-conscious that the tone and pitch of my voice was changing even as I spoke. I could only imagine the look on his face as it did so. My eyes still closed, I maintained my calm centred self-control and, beginning the most difficult part of the transformation, changed my tweeds into a suitable dress for a young lady.

The esteem in which I hold seamstresses and tailors alike never ceases to rise whenever I attempt to do something like this. How they manage to create well-fitting fashionable garments with nothing more than a needle, thread and a few yards of cloth is something of which I shall ever be in awe. It is difficult enough by arcane means to hem a skirt correctly, let alone create a passable bustle.

When I opened my eyes, Forshaw looked alarmed, for which I cannot blame him. It is not every day a man changes their appearance to that of a young woman before your eyes. While it is true he'd seen me do other things one could consider miraculous with the mystic arts, a man taking on the appearance of a woman is perhaps philosophically more difficult to stomach than bolts of arcane energy emerging from his fingertips or him summoning phantoms with which to discourse.

It was also perhaps all the worse because Forshaw found Lucy Drake quite an attractive young woman from the somewhat scarlet pallor my companion suddenly exhibited.

"I say, Lucifer, this is…" he started in a tone that suggested some protest would be forthcoming.

As such, I decided to cut his protestations short. "It's Lucy… Lucy Drake… Miss Drake, if you will be so kind. Mr Forshaw. Best to set that name in your mind right now, but honestly, my friend, it is merely glamour magic, the like of which I know you have seen before."

"Seen before… Dash it, man, I may have seen it before but… A young lady… Why it's…"

"A convenience is what it is. We need to find out who is pulling Hendriks' strings and while you are known as an acquaintance of mine, you are also known to enjoy the company of young women."

"Enjoy the company of young women. What are you trying to imply?" he blustered.

"Oh Forshaw, my dear chap, I imply no impropriety, you are known by all to be nothing but a perfect gentleman. But you are also known to have escorted many a debutant on forays into society, tea dances, balls, the races and what have you. No one will be in the least surprised at your escorting young Miss Drake to tea at The Lords Pavilion. You are a member after all." I reminded him of this last nugget. Forshaw for his many graces had a blind spot when it came to cricket.

He actually enjoys the damn fool sport.

"A member… Yes, indeed, but still, this seems…"

"It's merely glamour magic."

"Glamour magic."

"Indeed, and nothing more than that."

"Nothing more than that…" he said. His visage took on a thoughtful façade for a moment, then he added, with a speculative tone. "Dashed impressive though, I must say, from what I've read, glamour magic requires time to prepare and cast. Why, you've told me as much in the past. Yet you made it seem so effortless, and…"

"We've been riding this cab quite a while, Forshaw. I have been preparing for this spell since we entered it," I lied. He was right, of course. Glamour magic takes time to cast, but I felt no need to burden him with the details of how I managed to change so swiftly. I felt it better that he just assumed I'd been preparing for the transformation the whole journey, better by far in fact than my explaining just how I became Lucy Drake before his eyes in a matter of moments.

The members' pavilion at Lords is, one must allow, well-appointed for a sports club. While the upper floor is of course for gentlemen only, the lower floor tearooms ran the length of the pavilion. It was a marvel of architectural engineering in many regards. The tearooms were spacious, but every few yards iron columns, painted white, extended between the floor and the ceiling, supporting the weight of the floors above through a steel subframe. In effect the whole building was a framework of steel with the walls built in afterwards. Think of it as an elaborate cage…

All that iron, I may add, played merry hell with my aetheretic senses.

Forshaw, playing his role in our deception for all it was worth, escorted me from the cab, through the pavilion's main entrance into the tearooms, with a degree of gallantry that surprised me. He even went so far as to pull out a chair for me at the table we were led to. All the while he managed to exchange greetings with several fellow cricket enthusiasts as we progressed through the room, one or two of whom raised an eyebrow at him or stared a little too long in our direction. Forshaw was after all a man in his early forties while I was for all appearance's sake a woman twenty years his junior. I heard at least one of his acquaintances mutter something along the lines of 'lucky bugger' when we were beyond ear shot.

Which, I may add, we certainly were not.

I also noted that this all seemed to delight Forshaw a little too much, in my opinion.

From the occasional whooping shouts and cheering beyond the windows, I surmised the game was progressing, though I declined the opportunity to turn around and seek out the scoreboard beyond the glass panes. I was however intent on letting my gaze sweep the tearoom, whence it fell on our prey. Indeed, as luck would have it, he was directly in my eye line, once I was seated.

"Tea, my dear?" Forshaw asked as I stared over his shoulder at Hendricks who was standing with three other gentlemen by the large bay windows, observing the match. They were, I noticed, standing quite rigidly and whatever was going on in the game beyond the window seemed to entice no reaction from any of them.

In fairness, this meant nothing, it was a cricket match out there, after all.

I nodded back to my companion, whose expression was much like that of an itinerant schoolboy out stealing apples. He was enjoying our charade a little too much.

We sat for several minutes, drinking tea and engaging in polite conversation, conversation not at all like that in which we normally engaged. Mostly, Forshaw spoke and I nodded or agreed with him. Playing the sheltered debutant, a young lady with little knowledge of the world, politics or much else. A parody of young womanhood... which is to say I played what society expected a young woman to be, rather than what young women are. An act for which I felt a certain shame. This act did however enable me to watch the three gentlemen by the window and as I watched I became more convinced with each passing minute that Hendricks was not the only walking corpse in attendance. They may as well have been a trio of tailor's dummies for all the life they exhibited.

"Forshaw, we don't see you down here as often as we should," said a voice I recognised, approaching the table, "and who, prey tell, is this delightful young lady with you?"

I turned my gaze away from my quarry and found myself looking up at Sir William Clayton, who as you may know, happened to be Private Secretary to the Home Office and, I may add, a buffoon when not at his desk. He was also in my experience an unconscionable bore on any subject save politics, which due to his professionalism he would never discuss. Personally, I had little time for the man, but he and Forshaw maintained a friendship forged in desperate circumstance. This is to say they attended boarding school together. As such, he was a friend by acquaintance and given his political clout a useful one. He was, however, also the last person I'd have chosen to engage with right at that moment as for a private secretary he had a voice like a foghorn and the tact of a fleet of ironclads being sent up the Yellow River to negotiate a trading concern.

By virtue of his voice alone, he was drawing attention our way.

"If I may present Miss Lucy Drake, the cousin of a mutual acquaintance," Forshaw replied in a tone that verged on the surreptitious towards the end. He could not be more obvious that he was up to something if he'd tried.

Clayton gave me a quizzical looking over, fleetingly looked back at Forshaw, then back at me. Then he held out his hand to accept my own in gentlemanly fashion. "Miss Drake, I believe I detect a little of your cousin in your eyes. How is our dear queen's favourite magician?"

"Cousin Lucifer is quite well, I believe. Busy as ever with his distractions. He absolutely deplores cricket unfortunately, so he imposed on poor Mr Forshaw to accompany me to the game. William was most kind to agree," I said, laying my hand on his and doing what passed for a polite curtsey, when a lady is seated, which amounts to little more than a nod of the head in his direction.

While I had neither the desire, nor intent, as Lucy, to play the wide-eyed debutant, I must admit it had it uses. Clayton looked suitably charmed and bowed to me lightly in return.

It was then I felt a familiar tingle in the air. A slight, almost imperceivable shifting in the aether, as Clayton's hand held my own and he leaned in to kiss it lightly. This caught me by surprise, coming as it was from a bore like Clayton, but I knew at once what had occurred. It was a minor detection spell of some order, yet as soon as I felt it, it was gone. I managed to mask my surprise with a girlish smile, easily mistaken for glee at the courtly nature of his manners.

I shall not pretend to be pleased with myself for doing so.

Releasing my hand, Clayton righted himself as he took out his pocket watch and pressed the catch to open it. He then seemed to take a moment or two to examine the time, while failing to mask a look of mild surprise. I suspected the watch was the source of the spell I had felt a moment before. In effect, it was a residual meter. As such, I had to fight the urge to smile once more. I had caught him looking for a glamour, which suggested the old bore was not quite as dim as I supposed.

Devices such as the residual meter I deduced his pocket watch to be are unfortunately far from uncommon. While I was surprised that he possessed one, I perhaps should not have been. As a high ranking official in Victoria Sax Coburg's government, he could doubtless afford such devices and a means to detect magic in your vicinity when you lacked the gift yourself doubtless had its uses. Luckily, however, if one has the talent, time and energy to perfect a glamour then one can easily subvert such things. Only the hastiest of magical disguises would set such a device off.

If it detected anything magical in nature about my appearance at all, it would be minor. The kind of background residue you would detect from a broach or such, that had the kind of harmless little glamours to enhance a lady's smile or disguise laughter lines. Cosmetic enchants of the kind sold in well-to-do jewellers throughout the city.

Closing his watch, Clayton looked at me with a new and quite different interest. I was, I am sure, according to his device, no more than I appeared. To wit, a pretty young woman of marriageable age. His smile became, I felt, a little lecherous at that point.

Something I pretended not to notice, in the fashion of young ladies everywhere.

"Well, Miss Drake, I'm delighted to make your acquaintance. But one must pursue the interests of Her Majesty's Government, sadly. Perhaps if you are free to attend the Season, we might cross paths again?" he inquired, in a way that lacked any subtly as to my, that is Lucy's, status. I half expected him to fish in his pocket for a card in the hopes of obtaining my own. Which is something of a game among bachelors of a certain type in London.

Forshaw saved my blushes, so to speak, by offering his own hand to Clayton.

"Damn fine to see you as ever, Clayton. We must catch up properly one of these days," he said, with a protective, verging on possessive tone, one intended to suggest that Lucy Drake was his prize, and Clayton would do well to back off. Which suggests he is a better actor than I give him credit for at times. Clayton seemed to take this none too subtle hint and with a shake of Forshaw's hand left us to it.

Forshaw chuckled to himself, and I failed entirely not to chuckle with him, as we watched Clayton withdraw. But it was where he went next that reinvigorated my interest in him. He stalked across the tearoom towards Hendrick and his statue-like companions by the window. Thence he began talking to them in hushed tones quite unlike those I associated with his normal tactless grandiloquence.

Forshaw noticed this too and shot me an inquiring eye.

I was tempted, so very tempted, to weave a touch of air magic. A minor alteration spell can create vortices in the air that will carry sound. I believe I first came across the trick in one of Newton's journals. Sir Isaac, true to form, gave it the ludicrous name of 'Newton's Ear', which conjures up images of some spectral appendage, when all it really involves is a manipulation of basic physical laws to carry audible vibrations over a short distance. But simple though such a spell usually was, in the iron frame of the pavilion it could easily go awry.

There was also a chance that casting the spell might set off Clayton's pocket watch. For a spell designed for listening in to whispered conversations from afar it is, in magical terms at least, annoyingly loud. As most manipulations directed outward rather than inward tend to be. Regretfully I dismissed the notion and instead fell back on other means to achieve my aim. This is to say I listened as carefully as I could to try and catch what was being said, while trying to read the lips of Hendricks and the others, as Clayton had his back to me. Reading lips is, I know, terribly mundane, but you would be surprised how often the mundane is as effective, if not more so, than actual magic. Something I discovered quite early in my career.

I have always found this somewhat disappointing, personally. You study a magical spell for months on end in order to animate a broom, then you realise it's more effective to just pick up the damn thing and sweep the floor yourself. Such is the tragedy of mages…

I caught enough of what passed between the men, more than enough in fact, as Clayton led Hendricks and the others past our table and across to the staircase that led to the upper floor. Up there were the private members' rooms which are often used for meetings about things other than willow on leather.

Or, occasionally so I am told, for a different kind of willow swung against a different kind of leather.

"Time for us to go," I told Forshaw.

"Go? But are we not going to take in a little of the game first?" he asked, which caused me to exhale with annoyance.

"No, my dear chap, 'sadly' there is little time for cricket."

"Little time for cricket? I say. Then what's afoot, Mandrake?" he said, though at least he had the common grace to hush his voice first before using my given name.

All the same, I gave him a hard stare for this slip and gestured to the effect it was time for him to escort Miss Drake from the tearooms, saying nothing until we were in a cab once more heading across London to my apartment off Baker Street.

"What's afoot is treason, or at the very least a design to subvert Her Majesty's Government," I told him. Then pointedly refused to go into more details. Least ways in a London cab. I felt it unwise to tell him I had gleaned but a few words from broken sentences, 'witchcraft bill,' 'the vote', 'Earnest to maintain the status quo' were about the extent of what I had gleaned. It was however the last words I caught that put a real shiver down my spine, which were, 'as His Majesty wishes'.

I could have misread. Reading lips is far from an exact science. But I feared I had read the words just as they were spoken. That 'his' was a word to shake the foundations of Great Britain. A queen sat on the throne, for the first time since Queen Anne. As such, no man, not even the prince consort, had claim to the title Majesty. My fears over the fate of the witchcraft bill were as nothing compared to the possibility of some pretender seeking primacy in the court of Saint James but that was not the worst of it.

The worst of it was that word 'Earnest'. I had not heard the word, only read it on the lips of a dead man. But rather than professing an earnestness to maintain the status quo it could just as easily have been 'Ernest to maintain the status quo'.

There was one Ernest I could think of to whom the honorific Majesty could be afforded, and that was the person of the King of Hanover. The other throne that had been denied our Queen Victoria due to her gender. There had been those who had professed the point of view that Earnest of Hanover should also have been handed the British throne ahead of his cousin, and he may have been but for the unpopularity of his father the Duke of Cumberland.

The implications of Ernest of Hanover meddling in British affairs were too dark to contemplate. Not least because one of the many reasons his father had been unpopular was a firm view on the restriction of the mystical arts to those who historically had right to wield them.

We alighted at Baker Street and Forshaw continued his role as escort to take me to my door. There I bid him good-day and made my way to my apartments to consider what little we had learned. By rights, it was my duty to report what I had gleaned to high office. But the involvement of Clayton, Private Secretary to Sir Robert Peel, worried at me. Was the Home Secretary involved somehow in all this? It didn't seem possible. Sir Robert had always publicly been a stanch supporter of the Queen. He was a royalist to the core. It occurred to me, however, a royalist he may be, but he was one that had been known to complain about 'that wilful woman' to me on more than one occasion privately, when talking of the Queen.

I had always thought such words were no more than the vented frustrations of a loyal subject, but perhaps there was more to it. Perhaps he was a royalist who would prefer to see a king upon the Westminster throne when it came to the state opening of parliament each year. It seemed hard to countenance such an idea, but Peel was a political animal at heart. Could I afford to dismiss the possibility?

No, I reasoned, I could not take this to Sir Robert, not yet. Not without more proof than a few words read from the lips of a dead man, and more certainty about his lack of involvement.

The lips of a dead man… there was that too. Someone was practising necromancy. An art that even in these enlightened days was considered suspect. Someone powerful. Powerful enough that they could risk acting in the open. Raising dead Lords from the grave to affect a vote in the house, it was almost too brazen.

Considering all this, I sat and took a brandy and for

a while stared across the room into the mirror at Lucy Drake's reflection. She was a useful ploy, my dearest Lucy. A simple girl unfettered by intrigue and dubious reputation. But it was not Lucy Drake who was going to untangle this web.

Finishing the brandy, I began the careful breathing exercises as I focused upon the image before me, glad that my housekeeper knew enough to leave me undisturbed for several hours at a time. I focused my gaze on Lucy's eyes.

Eyes that were my own, after all.

You'll remember I said I lied to Forshaw at the end of the cab ride to Lords. That I told him I'd been focusing on the glamour I'd cast since we entered the cab. Such a facile lie, I was surprised even dear gullible Forshaw accepted it at face value. A truly complete glamour takes longer than a twenty-minute cab ride, and wheels bouncing over cobblestones do little to aid focus on such magics.

A true glamour, an impenetrable glamour carefully constructed to fool any but the most skilled magician and certainly fool such trinkets as Clayton had employed... such a glamour takes hours to cast and slip into.

As I stared into Lucy Drake's eyes, they changed slightly, as did the face staring back at me. Slowly over the course of an hour or more, the face changed from that of Lucy Drake to that with which I chose to face the world. The face of Lucifer Mandrake.

Mandrake, my own little joke, to keep me smiling.

You see, a glamour takes hours to case and perfect. Dropping one, however?

Why, you can drop a glamour in a moment, no matter how much the cab rattles over the cobblestones of London.

THE ASPIDISTRA OF SOCIAL INEQUALITY

If perchance you've never found yourself attempting to look inconspicuous on an underground platform at two in the morning, while cradling a potted aspidistra under one arm, furtively glancing towards the representative of Her Majesty's constabulary stood beside the ticket office, you should consider yourself lucky.

Should you be so unlucky as to find yourself in such a position, however, then you should offer a silent prayer of thanks to whatever gods you hold dear if your previously unwisely tight trousers haven't developed a severe case of improved ventilation. To be a tad more specific, that you hadn't caught them on a railing spike while evading a different officer of the Queen's peace, while juggling with the potted plant I mentioned earlier.

Indeed, if I may further advise, if to your chagrin your chosen deity doesn't intercede so that his pious believer treads a different path than one that leads to an underground platform, at two in the morning, in ripped trousers, carrying an aspidistra, and seeking to evade London's finest… Then at the very least pray that he grants you the wisdom to follow this path while sober, rather than after drinking the better part of a bottle of finest London gin. Or mediocre but affordable London gin at any rate…

Though why anyone would do such a thing sober is beyond me.

Regardless of your sobriety or otherwise, however, let me offer one final piece of advice on the matter. If perchance one does find oneself on an underground platform, at 2am, drunk, in exceptionally ventilated trousers, trying to avoid catching the eye of the copper by the ticket office, at the very least make sure the potted plant is potted in a plant pot, as opposed to some other receptacles that could conceivably be used for such a purpose.

I mention this last for no particular reason...

Now in my defence, it has to be said, what I happened to be using as a plant pot was at least a reasonable substitute. That is as long as you're happy carrying the plant in question. Admittedly it wouldn't serve as a long-term method of housing said plant. The rounded end, with its nipple like silver cap, wouldn't stand up on its own, which is something of a flaw as far as acting as a plant pot is concerned. This, however, was a moot point, for otherwise as a receptacle for carrying an aspidistra across the fair city of London, it was more or less perfect.

Unfortunately, all considered, I suspected the member of London's finest by the ticket office was likely to take issue with my choice of plant pot all the same. As such, despite all the courage inspired by the quarter pint of mediocre London dry I had partaken of earlier that evening, the situation in which I found myself was making me a tad nervous. Needless to say, were the officer at the ticket office to precede to feel my collar, I was honour bound to maintain that none of this unfortunate situation was in fact my fault. Indeed, I would argue, some would say I was utterly blameless...

They would be wrong of course, but I consider that too was a somewhat moot point.

Let me be honest here, so there is no lie between

us, at this juncture at any rate. I must admit I had purloined the aspidistra. I'll also admit that the doing of this felonious act had required scaling the fences at the Royal Horticultural Show in Chelsea. Fences made of iron railings with an unfortunate array of spikes on their crest. I will also admit to doing this after a protracted drinking session down the Fulham Road, which was the reason I was a tad unsteady on my feet and caught the seat of my trousers on those delightfully sharp railings. Hence the excessive ventilation of my posterior. I feel however some background might be in order here. Nuance is always important, it's not like I habitually go around stealing flora. Despite a rather fraught but interesting relationship I once had with a girl called Rose, I'm no dendrophile.

I had a good reason for stealing this particular plant, A reason that stems from why I was drinking down the Fulham Road in the first place. In truth I'd been out on the lash with several members of 'The Ins and Outs'. Or to give it its official name 'The Naval, Air and Military Club', a gentleman's club in the moderately fashionable end of Soho, though no one ever referred to it by its official name. Members of 'The Ins and Outs' were men primarily in the armed services. The type of men who feel the need to occasionally blow off some steam in town. 'The Ins' was not quite as infamous as the Hellfire club and it was certainly less prestigious than the likes of Diogenes. It was, however, a young man's club, with a growing reputation for escapades its members referred to as 'high jinks'. Or 'loutish hooliganism' as more than one magistrate chose to describe the actions of club members dragged before them.

Suffice to say 'The Ins and Outs' was a club with a 'reputation' and its members were at best what my old gin-soaked mum would have called 'a load of bloody Hooray Henrys'. Which is to say the same kind of drunken, thuggish, gambling, womanisers she was used to seeing every day in the East End, but with family money, cut glass accents and second cousins.

I've noticed over the years that only the rich seem to have second cousins while the poor can barely afford the first ones. Though if you are part of certain East End families who tread a path on the grey side of legalities, you can have any number of uncles, like those of my old mate Frankie who held court at 'The Elves'.

In any regard, 'The Ins and Outs' was by all accounts a club full of wealthy hooligans with bad drinking habits and worse gambling problems. It seemed like my kind of club, primarily because drunken gamblers, particularly bad ones with lots of disposable cash, happen to be among my favourite people. This was one of the reasons I was keen to join.

The drinking session which led to me standing on that station platform had been by way of my introduction to a few of the members. It had, I must admit, been a good night and I felt sure I'd got myself well in with the lads. It was however also this night out that had led to me to nick the aspidistra from the Chelsea Flower Show. An act of creative larceny which was, not to blow my own tuba, something of a stroke of genius on my part. The kind of stroke of genius that strikes a man after the better part of a quart of gin. Which is to say, bloody idiocy...

It had however seemed a good idea at the time.

Now, you may be wondering why on earth I would

think nicking an aspidistra was a good idea, no matter how much gin I had poured down my neck. Well, the simplest explanation is that around that time in my life I'd developed a desire to improve my station. This was back when I was a freshly minted but somewhat lowly gunnery officer in Old Iron Knickers' Air Navy. Lowly being something of an understatement, as if the captain had a cat, I suspect the feline in question would have out-ranked me. My prospects for advancement were also limited. Despite being a graduate of The Royal Air and Naval Collage, I remained an orphan of the empire. A man without family or connections, and let us be completely frank about it, without an ounce of breeding. My education may have made an officer of me, but I was the kind of officer the empire expected to do or die, and mostly the latter, for her cause. My assets beyond my commission stretched to owning a decent pair of boots I'd obtained in somewhat odd, slightly felonious circumstances, and a hand tailored uniform that just about fit as the hand tailoring had to be done by yours truly. All of which amounted to this, I remained as the parlance of my peers at their most polite would sometimes put it, a pleb from the wrong side of the tracks.

In fairness, my peers were wrong. Where I'd been born, we looked upon those from the wrong side of the tracks with a degree of envy. We didn't have tracks to be on the wrong side of, all we had was ruts in the road that served as gutters, open sewers and occasionally as early graves.

Suffice to say, despite my commission Hannibal Smyth was still at heart Harry Smith. An orphan from the crappy end of East London. My family connections amounted to a mother who'd passed some ten years before and a father whose name, assuming she knew it, she had taken to her gin soaked grave. What little station I had in life was entirely down to my years as an orphan of the empire because someone somewhere had mistakenly gotten the idea that the father I never knew had been an officer killed on active service. But let's face it, Harry or Hannibal, it didn't matter, I had no family to speak of. Certainly not one that would help grease the wheels of advancement.

As for that other great lever of promotional prospects, the old school tie. Well, some may claim Ruggley School for Orphans of the Empire is a fine institution. They may also say educating the sons of the Empire's 'heroes' is a thing to be lorded. In reality, however, mostly it churned out the next generation of low-grade officers for Old Iron Knickers' gristle mill. Some few of my fellow 'Ruggers' with actual family connections might hope to carve out a career at Horse-Guards, but the majority of us took the first commission thrown our way and kept it for as long as we remained alive. Mostly, we sons of the Empire's heroes followed our fathers into early graves. If we were lucky, we'd get to spawn the next generation of sons before we did. In any regard, helping old school mates get a leg up isn't on the agenda of men spending all their time ducking bullets.

So a few low-ranking officers with prospects little better than my own were my old school tie, put like that and my lack of family connections and the prospects of Hannibal Smyth were no better than old Harry Smith's had been before I got dragged out of the East End. Saving that I now had a name that sounded like it belonged in the home counties and I could fake the right kind of accent. Something you learn to do when dropping H's is a good way to earn yourself a battering at Public School.

So you see, this was the reason for my overwhelming desire to join 'The Ins and Outs'. As an up-and-coming young gentleman's club for officers of all three services, it was ideal. Not least because its members believed themselves to be far more liberal than most. Liberal enough that my application had a hope in hell of being accepted.

Membership of 'The Ins and Outs', I hoped, would give me access to a better class acquaintance. I didn't expect to groom any actual friends there, but it would give me some decent contacts at least. Contacts that could lead to a more successful future for yours truly in service of old Iron Knickers. Well, it didn't quite work out that way, but that's a longer story as I'm sure you're aware. However, as with all such clubs, there was more to an application than just the formal process of writing to the membership committee.

This was how I came to be cradling an aspidistra in a makeshift pot plant, in torn trousers, on a draughty underground platform at 2am, blind drunk, trying not to attract the attention of Mr Plod.

This also, as it happens, caused me to have an epiphany.

Now, I'm aware that placing oneself in such a damn fool position before having an epiphany of any sort is bloody foolish. Epiphanies at 2am should take place beside a roaring fireplace, with a good brandy in one hand, a smouldering cigar in the other, and if you're particularly lucky, with a woman whose virtue you haven't had to negotiate, doing things to your trouser regions. Of course, such epiphanies as are granted in such circumstances are seldom entirely valid, but they are, I've found, often still the best ones.

My epiphany on the underground platform on the other hand was somewhat more prosaic if no less profound. An epiphany that surrounded what you might call the aspidistra of social inequality.

To explain further, my prospective club mates had charged me with the acquisition of a certain item by aberrant means. Said item, once acquired, had then to be taken from Chelsea, where the item was to be attained, across London to the doors of 'The Ins and Outs' in Soho where upon presenting said item I would gain entry to the members' bar.

There were rules of course. I wasn't allowed to hail a cab or use a water taxi for that matter. I was only allowed to use old shanks pony or such transport available to the general public for a sixpence or less. Trolly busses, underground trains, and the like. Very public transportation, as it were. The members, most of whom were of a class that would consider riding in 2nd class an exotic excursion into how the other half lived and were unaware such a thing as 3rd class existed, considered this rule hilarious. I suspect because they thought drunken tomfoolery would make you stand out on underground train in the early hours of the morning.

In addition, I had until dawn to present myself at the doors of the club, and had to do this while carrying the 'obtained item' openly and in full view. Quite specifically in full view of any members of the constabulary of our fair city. A final rule I was 'edging around', shall we say…

This was of course hijinks and all that. After all, it only involved a petty crime as crimes go. If caught, the most a prospective club member could expect to suffer as recrimination was an overnight lodging in the cells at Bow Street and a rap on the knuckles, figuratively speaking, from the magistrate the following morning. This, I suspect, was the whole point. They expected the prospective to get caught, that was the test as once caught you had to take your punishment while keeping tight lipped on any involvement in your crime of both the club and its members.

But there's the rub of it…

When old bill nick a toff, they're careful to make sure that toff doesn't accidentally slip down the stairs on the way to the ground floor cells. If you have a weak chin and Oxbridge accent, you don't as a rule feel the sweet kiss of a truncheon or three round the back of the head either. Coppers are scrupulously careful not to go roughing up a man whose father is likely to be on speaking terms with the commissioner. Chances are if you're a member of the weak chin brigade, before your arraignment the desk sergeant brings you a nice cup of tea, a bowl of warm water, and a cloth so you can clean yourself up. Then at your arraignment, the magistrate, who likely went to school with your father or knew someone who did, would make a broad speech on standards of behaviour expected of individuals like yourself, fine you fifty quid and have you escorted out the door. If he was in a bad mood, he might make it a hundred and threaten to have you locked up for a couple of days, though they would almost always suspend any sentence involved.

Basically, if your chin was weak enough, it really was just a rap on the knuckles.

On the other side of the coin however, if you're not a jobbing member of the rule class…. if your father didn't once play for the Cambridge second eleven… if instead your chin is of the fine jutting kind you could use as an anvil at a push and you're not on speaking terms with the Marquess of Gwent…Well, in that case, your experience of the justice system is going to be somewhat different.

Standing on that breezy platform, I realised if my collar was felt I'd almost certainly find myself falling down the stairs to the ground floor cells. I'd also be introduced to the business end of several truncheons either before or after my fall, and probably both. As for a cup of tea the morning after, well I doubt that would be in the offing and frankly the coppers were unlikely to give a damn if I was plastered in dried blood and had a black eye before I went up in front of the beak. As for the magistrates themselves… Well, as I was clearly an oink, they would hand out the maximum fine. A figure greater than whatever resided in my wallet, I was sure. I was almost assured to get a week or more in Wandsworth to boot and in all likelihood could kiss my brand-new commission goodbye into the bargain. Spending a week at Her Majesty's pleasure was frankly going to lead to the displeasure of Her Majesty's Royal Air Navy, so I'd probably also get a couple of months in the glass house for that, before being drummed out of the service for bringing dishonour to the uniform.

So, to sum up, my epiphany on the subject of social

inequality was this: it all comes down to who's holding the aspidistra…

It was about then, just as this realisation was sinking in, that to my relief I heard the tell-tale rushing sound of air pushed through a tunnel ahead of an approaching train. I stepped a little closer to the edge of the platform, risking a glance over at the representative of the Queen's peace, who thankfully seemed happy in his boredom and lacking any desire to have his interest piqued. Casually, I edged a little further down the platform and waited as the train erupted out of the mouth of the tunnel with the usual bellow of steam. I was still tempted to leave the damn plant, container and all, on a bench and blow the whole thing off as a fool's idea. Me being very much the fool in this regard. But I had gotten this far so it seemed currish not to follow through.

As the carriage doors lurched open, I steeled myself and stepped forward without checking the way was clear first. I blame the drink for that. In any regard, this led me to stumble straight into another damn copper, stepping out of the carriage as I was trying to climb aboard. I bluffed it out, smiling at him through the foliage of my aspidistra, mumbling a doubtlessly incoherent apology and stepped to one side to allow him to pass.

He grunted in my direction and turned down the platform without giving me a further glance. Which was lucky as I'd turned a shade of green to match the damn pot plant I was carefully cradling to my chest.

'I could always just leave it on the train,' I thought to myself after the desire to vomit through panic had passed, but again I found my resolve. There you see was the other rub of it all. If I got through this initiation, I'd a good chance of being made a member of the club. As a member of a Soho gentleman's club, well, that would stop me just being another pleb in the eyes of the law. It wasn't quite the protection afforded those born to wealth and status but it would make me 'born into wealth and status' adjacent in their eyes and afford me some leeway in future. It would open doors, offering me the glean of respectability... which has a certain irony as I also hoped it would prove useful with connections for my smuggling side-line. The one major advantage of being a gunnery officer was that the bomb bay had lots of places to hide contraband a man might want smuggled in and out of the country.

The doors of the train took their own sweet time in closing, affording me the chance to watch the two coppers chatting about something from my seat on the carriage. But eventually the doors swung shut once more and the train started to pull away. It was at this point a third copper, looking red-faced and flustered, his comb-over hair flapping freely in the breeze, rushed down the steps shouting. A sight which caused much hilarity for yours truly as I slumped down into a seat for the short hop of three stations before I could jump the train and walk the rest of the way. Call me petty by all means...

Somewhat later, but still an hour before dawn, having taken pains to avoid any more encounters with the boys in blue, I strode between the twin gates from which my prospective club got its name. Then, taking hold of the large brass knocker on the main entrance to 'The Ins and Outs', I rapped loudly on the door. As it was some time after 4am by this point, I will admit to being slightly surprised when a minute or so later as I was just about to reach for the brass knocker again, an aging gentleman in a doorman's uniform answered my summons and peered down a somewhat aquiline nose at my somewhat tattered visage.

"Yes?" came a haughty inquiry.

"I'm here to…" I started to say, before realising I actually had no idea what I needed to say. I mean, what do you say to the doorman of a gentleman's club at four in the morning when you're carrying an aspidistra. "Erm, Kenton," I managed.

The doorman continued to look down his nose at me for a moment, then nodded once before promptly shutting the door in my face.

I stood there before the entrance for several minutes. As I recall, it started to drizzle just to add to my woes, causing me to contemplate my life choices once more. I was about to just dump the plant on the steps and stalk off to my digs when the door opened once more and Kenton Ridgely-Scotsworth stepped out to join my bedraggled figure on the doorstep. Behind Kenton, several other club members, some of whom I had met while drinking earlier, were all crowded together, doubtless to have a good gawk at the pleb. There were others among them I did not recognise as well, a pudgy-looking cove with piggy little eyes, a haughty-looking swine in a uniform not unlike my own but with noticeably less ripped trousers, and surprisingly a rather buxom young woman holding a large whisky and making no attempt to hide her urge to laugh in my face.

I felt somewhat dreadful to be honest.

"Hannibal, isn't it?" Kenton said, though he knew

my damn name well enough. He was clearly playing up to the crowd behind him. All part of the hazing, no doubt.

"Yes," I managed, my normal eloquence deserting me momentarily. It had suddenly struck me that it was a distinct possibility my application to join 'The ins and Outs' was being treated as a joke by the members who were indeed now engaging in the age-old sport of putting a pleb in his place.

"Why, old boy, are you carrying a rubber plant?" Kenton asked me, with genuine bemusement in his voice. Behind him somebody, I suspect the one with the piggy little eyes, snickered.

"It's an aspidistra," I told him, a tad more defensively than I intended. I'd grown attached to that plant in the last few hours. I felt an overwhelming urge to defend its honour for some reason.

"I'll take your word for it, old chap, but that doesn't answer my question."

"It's… Well. It's for Kenton, just as you requested," I explained. This was true as it goes, though not exactly the plant itself.

"I'm afraid I don't follow you, old…" he started saying then his eyes lit up as he realised what I was using for a plant pot.

It was at this point he burst out laughing. "By God, you actually did it. Have you seen this? No one has ever made it back before!" he said, sounding genuinely impressed. He took the aspidistra and its improvised plant pot from my hands, holding it out to show the others with a look of triumph about him. He set himself marching back through the crowd and up to the umbrella stand by the foot of the main staircase where he planted the police constable's helmet, aspidistra and all, in it for all to see.

A cheer broke out among the members, who promptly all marched off in the direction of the bar, the buxom young woman gifting me a sly sort of smile into the bargain as they left me still standing there on the doorstep, soaked to the skin, in tattered trousers.

The doorman looked down his nose at me once again, handed me a towel, and with a tilt of his head beckoned me through the door.

I was, it seemed, in…

FIN

ABOUT THE AUTHOR

Author of the Hannibal Smyth Misadventures, The Ballad of Maybes series and his first two books, Passing Place and Cider Lane, Mark Hayes writes novels that often defy simple genre definitions; they could be described as speculative fiction, though Mark would never use the term as he prefers not to speculate.

He is also a messy, complicated sort of entity, a quantum pagan and occasional were-goth.

He said to say that he knows where his spoon is and to ask, do you?

He did not explain why this was important.

You can find out more at Markhayesblog.com.

Printed in Great Britain
by Amazon